The

DIAMOND
TALISMAN

A NOVEL

BY

SUSAN LANCASTER

Lancaster, Susan.
The diamond talisman
ISBN 0-9730350-0-5
I. Title.
    PS8573.A51D52 2002 jC813'.6 C2002-910071-2
    PZ7.L2208Di 2002

This novel is a work of fiction. Names, characters, places and incidents are either the product of the author's imagination or are used fictitiously. Any resemblance to actual persons living or dead, events or locales is entirely coincidental.

This book was published by:
SNOSRAP Publishing
P.O. Box 37039
3200 Island Highway
Nanaimo, B.C.
Canada V9T 1W0

e-mail: sanden@telus.net
www.snosrappublishing.com

Manufactured by:

Little Mountain Publishing

Parksville, B.C.
www.LittleMountainPublishing.com

Printed in Canada

This book is for

Caitlin,

Mary, Sarah and Raelyn

With love

Author's Note

I offer many grateful thanks to Richard Molnar, Dorothy Cella, Suzanne Ouimet, Wendy-Lynne MacKinnon and Gary Moore for their invaluable comments and input.

Gillian Borthwick and Doreen Besharah provided needed editorial ideas and assistance which was much appreciated.

Gratitude to Mike Molnar for some wonderfully creative artwork and Iain Parsons for his research assistance.

Last, but not least to Denis — a powerhouse of inspiration and encouragement - with love and thanks.

Table of Contents

— Chapter One —

The Deed Is Done

"Cor, what a beaut!" exclaimed Fingers, almost forgetting to keep his voice down as he stared at the exposed shimmering areas of the centuries-old diamond that lay in the palm of his gloved hand. Caught by the moonlight which streamed through the window on the left of him, the rough, uncut gem glistened and glinted in rainbow hues as Fingers and The Cat marvelled at it. This was the crowning glory of a long and successful career as a cat burglar and Fingers was not about to let the moment slip by.

Aptly named because of his long, claw-like, double-jointed fingers now encased in a kid glove, Fingers, otherwise known as Reggie Lund, peered down with a glint of satisfaction in his dark eyes. A wizard at the technicalities of opening safes, vaults and anything else which sported a lock, Fingers was a man of few words, simple thinking and plain speech. However, when the job was done, he was quite capable of savouring the spoils and indulging in self-appreciation. A hint of a smirk was visible on his mouth and his skeletal frame seemed to sway, almost to a slow dance of victory as he contemplated the sparkling gem.

In the meantime his friend The Cat, otherwise known as Tim Bowden, after initially taking in the beauty and potential value of the diamond, set about much more practical matters, by removing the remaining contents of the safe. The Cat was the thinker and planner of the partnership and was well aware of Finger's tendency to either waste time gloating when things went right or to panic if they went wrong. Like Fingers, he was aptly named because his body echoed the grace and movement associated with our feline friends. In addition to The Mirendah Diamond, there was diamond, ruby and emerald jewellery, some of the gold and silver settings indicating the age of the pieces, handed down from generation to generation. The Cat didn't doubt that the street value would be enormous.

Checking that he had emptied the safe, The Cat put his hand right to the back and touched what felt like a small package, which he gradually eased out. The light of his torch depicted numbers and the word 'Bearer' on one of the pieces of paper. "They must be bonds," he thought to himself as he turned the package over and discovered that the Issuer was The County Mercantile Bank. "Very old and valuable – and what's more, they aren't even made out to anyone in particular – what a break," mused The Cat to himself as he placed them with the other jewellery.

The room and house seemed eerily quiet as Fingers worked to relock the safe that was set in the wall behind a big old-fashioned wardrobe. The bedroom in which the safe was housed was huge and the moonlight created an almost eerie glow on the priceless bedspread and wall hangings. The stillness and the light combined to provide an atmosphere that could easily conjure up ghosts with clanking chains, but the only sound to be heard was a muffled, uneven thud-thud as Fingers and The Cat dragged the large wardrobe back in front of the safe. All they had to do now was to collect their tools and spoils and get out of there as quickly as possible. But Fingers was still in such an excited state over the diamond that The Cat was finding it very difficult to bring him back to reality!

"I just knew it," bellowed Roger Corr as he paced to and fro, one fist banging into the palm of the other hand as he ranted and raged. "Those lowdown rats, how dare they double cross me! No one ever does that – do your hear, Max – no one!" His audience of one agreed – in fact he would agree with anything seeing Roger in this state. Most dangerous!

Roger Corr was the mastermind behind the notorious Corr Gang, renowned for their very clever and untraceable cat burglaries and for the intimidation of any shady underworld character who dared to question Roger in any way. Roger was also wanted for the odd gangland murder. There was no doubt that the police would almost trade in their badges to catch this small, unassuming, bespectacled man with a moustache and Charlie Chaplin bowler hat. But behind the mask of respectability was a cunning, cruel and ruthless character who had long ago, when adopting his hat, laid the seed for his life of crime. Like the two sides of his character, his moods swung from coolness to towering rage from one minute to the next and none of his fellow gang members knew when it was going to happen.

And this was what Max, one of his two trusty lieutenants, was witnessing now. He did not see the mild, unassuming man before him, but a raging monster, bent on the destruction of Fingers and The Cat. Ever since Roger had heard the rumour that his two colleagues were planning to double-cross him and go it alone after the robbery he had planned at Ryerdale Hall, he had been beside himself with rage.

The Hall had been the seat of the Marquesses of Ryerdale for the past four centuries. The present Lord Ryerdale was currently on holiday for six weeks in his villa on Grand Bahama

Island, little knowing that his absence was the opportunity for the robbery of the century. A heist painstakingly masterminded, researched and planned by Roger Corr and carried out by his two most outstanding cat burglars, Fingers and The Cat.

Ryerdale Hall is nothing short of a medieval castle. Built in 1431, it was originally a fortified manor house, occupied by minor royal descendents of the then defunct Principality of North Wales. It continued as a manor house for sometime, ownership changing hands over the years and was purchased from one of the descendents by John, Lord Ryerdale in 1585. Lord John was Lord Keeper of the Great Seal, a popular courtier and a member of the Queen's inner circle. Following Lord John's purchase of Ryerdale Hall, he was gifted by the Queen with extensive lands running parallel to the property he had purchased, which was not insubstantial in itself. Later, in recognition of further services at Court he was elevated to the title of Marquess. This position, together with his vast land holdings, now justified a house that would reflect his status. Thus, work was begun on the manor house to turn it into a building resembling a castle with the addition of a Keep and castellated walls. These renovations and extensions took many years and were not completed until approximately 1660 by Rupert, the grandson of John Ryerdale.

As it was finished, so it has stood, just as there has been no interrupted ownership of the Hall. No more work was done to change the outside appearance of the Hall, except of course for maintenance, and it wasn't until the late 19th century that further work was undertaken to modernize the buildings to bring them into the 20th century. The Hall is positioned at the top of a small knoll and the impressive sandstone of the castle dominates the surrounding pastural countryside as it stands amid several thousand acres of land. Much of the land is now leased to nearby farmers, although the current Marquess, Lord Andrew, retained about 15,000 acres for farming himself that is delegated to his estate manager. The parkland is also used for exercising horses belonging to the Marshioness who is an accomplished equestrienne, encouraging the use of the side-saddle for riding.

The Hall is divided into three separate areas. The central, and the largest of the three areas contains all the State Rooms used throughout generations for entertaining, socializing and hospitality. On the ground floor is the entrance gallery situated behind the massive oak doors that protect the Hall from the outside world. The entrance gallery leads directly to the Great Hall, complete with Minstrel Gallery, where many years of feasts and dancing had been held. It is seldom used now, but looking down on the Great Hall from the Gallery, it is easy to imagine the gentlemen of the past in their uniforms and the ladies dancing with their long, flowing dresses dipping and swaying; the air filled with the sound of music while the light from a myriad of candles was reflected in the fabulous jewels worn by the ladies.

Various exits from the Great Hall lead to other rooms in the Central complex which also house the library, the drawing room, the dining room, the breakfast room and a reception area. Upstairs are the State bedrooms, especially reserved for the elite of the land when they visited and in the Ryerdale's case, visitors have included three reigning monarchs over the centuries.

The building to the left of the central block was The Keep that contained the family apartments, spread out over the three floors. In contrast to the magnificent old wall hangings, curtains and uncomfortable furnishings of bygone days that prevail in the central block of state rooms, the décor and furnishing of the family apartments is a pleasant eclectic mix of ancient, modern and not so modern style decoration. For example, in the master bedroom, there are some of the luxurious hangings around the four poster bed and windows, normally found in the state rooms. These blend with modern style chairs and carpets. In turn this is balanced by huge old armoires and chests of drawers. The overall impression is one of beauty and comfort because the different styles work together in a large room to produce a spectacular impression.

To the right of the central block are the various and many offices belonging to the managers of functions which keep the Hall, farm and estates operating smoothly. This block has a lower ground floor which houses a Stables Court and Yard, last used when horses and carriages were the only mode of transport. Also located on the lower ground floor is a Kitchen Court that used to house all the domestic activities of the Hall. Only the large kitchen remains and many of the now unnecessary smaller rooms surrounding the kitchen, such as the Coal Vault, The Still Room, The Pastry Room and others have been converted into modern offices for current staff and supervisors. One of the rooms is the hub for the Hall's closed-circuit television system. This operations room is manned for eighteen hours a day, seven days a week. To supplement the closed-circuit television network is a highly sophisticated alarm system which is activated for the remaining six hours at night and alerts the local police station if anything goes amiss.

Roger Corr had discovered that when the Marquess was

at home, the Kitchen Court was a hive of activity, but when he was on one of his extended holidays, the staff complement was severely reduced. In fact, at night there were only three men on duty in the house, although the systems are wired to the local police station for back-up if needed. Roger had also established that until eleven o'clock at night, the Hall was monitored by the closed circuit sets only. The automatic alarm system had motion detectors in every conceivable part of The Hall and could not be activated prior to eleven o'clock at night because of the number of people coming and going within The Hall up to that time.

Historically, the Ryerdale family home had been a house of intrigue down through the years, providing much fuel for gossip and legend amongst the local villagers – indeed, the tales were sometimes shocking enough to reach the nearest town thirteen miles away. What was not generally known was that the present Marquess of Ryerdale was the owner of some fabulously valuable jewels, some of which had been passed on by various members of the family and others that had been acquired by sometimes dubious methods. Amongst these was the famous Mirendah Diamond.

The Mirendah was an unusual stone, dating back several centuries before the art of polishing and cutting diamonds was discovered. It is a 'rough', uncut diamond worn as a talisman in the past because it was said to have many magical, mystical and medicinal properties. It was also rumoured to be the missing half of the famous Cullinan Diamond. The Cullinan Diamond is the largest gem quality diamond ever discovered and when it was originally found some signs on it suggested that that it may have been part of a much larger diamond. The missing half has never been discovered.

Prized in the past more for its mystical qualities rather than its value, the stone eventually ended up in the possession of the Sultan of Mirendah, from whom it was stolen in 1867 by Cecil, the then heir to Ryerdale Hall. Cecil had arranged for 'windows' to be polished on the girdle of the stone, in order to see if there were any flaws. This was enough to allow the Ryerdales and their diamond specialists to assess the real, staggering value of the clear, brilliant stone. It was also what caused Fingers and The Cat to gasp in awe at the treasure that the actual, polished stone would become.

All this, of course, helped to explain why the diamond had never seen the light of day and why only a few people knew of its existence. Although this handful of people did not include either the police or the insurance companies, it did now include Roger Corr. He knew the polishing and cutting of the stone would easily change the shape and identity of the diamond and it would be easier to dispose of the newly cut stone. Therein lay the value for Roger Corr. He knew full well that he would only have one crack at getting this stone so he had to get it right the first time. After months of preparation he had detailed Fingers and The Cat to carry out the job. They were exceptionally fit and agile. They were also perfectionists. The Cat had both intelligence and common sense and Fingers provided the technical know-how. They made an excellent team.

The jewels were kept in a safe in Lord and Lady Ryerdale's bedroom, part of the family apartments located in the Keep. The Keep stood to the left of the main building. Access to it was via a ground floor passageway from the main building. The master bedroom was at the end of The Long Gallery on the second floor, but Fingers and The Cat had to get to it via the balcony of the Blue Room, on the west side of the Keep, so as not to be overlooked by any other part of the Hall. To get to the balcony meant some difficult climbing by rope, but that was something the two of them were quite used to doing on a regular basis.

Now Roger felt that all his plans might come to nothing as he thought of all he would like to do to Fingers and The Cat if he could get his hands on them. All the cool reason used in his planning evaporated when he suddenly shouted ferociously that Max must stop the two men at all costs. Max obeyed without question although he knew deep down it was absolute madness to try and stop the robbery, especially since there were only two hours left before Fingers and The Cat would arrive at the Hall to start the job. Furthermore, he and Roger were in Manchester and Ryerdale Hall was in North Wales, at least a good two and a half hour journey away. However, at least agreeing to go would get him away from Roger, who had now become as angry as Max had ever seen him.

The robbery was timed to occur in the late evening, one hour before the security alarms were activated. Through careful study Roger had discovered that only one man is left in the television 'operations' room from nine o'clock, while the other two security men rest in the staffs' private quarters. Roger had decided this was the time that Fingers and The Cat should attempt the robbery because it is the quietest time, security-wise.

All had gone according to plan and the two robbers scaled the walls of The Keep as they made their way up to the balcony outside the Blue Room. It took Fingers only a few minutes to carefully pick the lock on the french doors. After they were through the doors, Fingers made sure that the rope was still in place and that the doors were just pulled to – a necessity for a quick getaway. Both of them had been fully briefed by Roger on the location of the TV camera for the Long Gallery, which was directly above the door of the Blue Room looking down the centre and the right-hand side of the Gallery. This meant that Fingers and The Cat could come through the Blue Room door and go along the wall at the left-hand side of the Gallery to the Master Bedroom door without being seen.

Max drove at breakneck speed to Ryerdale Hall, trying to think of a way to find and stop Fingers and The Cat. It was not going to be easy, especially since he had not been included in most of Roger Corr's planning meetings. He felt that the best policy was to find the rope they had used and scale the walls to the balcony. He would then position himself outside the door of the master bedroom and stop them when they came out. He felt the comfort of his pistol in its holster under his jacket and became a little less tense.

He arrived just after half past nine and parked his car well into the bushes on the country lane that went all round the grounds of the Hall. He scaled the outer wall and crossed the grounds to the west side of the Keep. He dared not use his torch, so he had to walk close to the walls of the Keep until he came upon the outline of the rope used by the other two. Agile Max was not, and it was with a lot of huffing and puffing he finally reached the french doors on the balcony, only to find them closed. He nearly had a fit – "all that for nothing," was his immediate thought. Still panting from his climb he decided to try the doors anyway, and found to his surprise that they were open, leaving him free and clear to enter.

Max had not anticipated the next problem which beset him – where precisely was the master bedroom? He knew it was either on the second or third floor. Since he was already on the second floor, he chose to explore that first. As he went into the Long Gallery and saw how many doors he would have to try in order to find the room he wanted, any thoughts he may have had about looking out for TV cameras went clean out of his head and he started on the doors along the right-hand side.

Burt Manley was the security man assigned to monitor the closed-circuit televisions that night. It had been a long day and Burt was tired. In fact he wanted nothing more than to return to his own room and put his feet up. He was nearly sixty years old, with many years of loyal and dedicated service to the Ryerdale Family behind him. He was rather a solid, jovial looking man with his hair definitely receding. He had a kind, ruddy coloured face with a hint of amusement in his eyes. Burt always looked at the most pessimistic of situations with a great deal of optimism which was just as well because he had found himself on a new high learning curve when the closed-circuit system was installed and there was a lot to learn about high-tech equipment. It was like starting life all over again but with Burt's positive attitude he had done surprisingly well and usually enjoyed checking the monitors. Tonight, though, because he was tired it had become a chore and besides, there was a football match he would rather have been watching.

As he was wondering what the final score of the match would be, his attention was captured by a figure, with its back to the camera, moving quite quickly along the Long Gallery in the Keep, opening, looking into and then closing the door of each room he came to. "That looks like Dale. What the heck is he doing up there at this time of night?" muttered Burt, "I'd better go and have a look see." Because he was so tired and it was nearly eleven o'clock, he didn't think to call for Stuart to come and cover the system before he left the room. It did not take him long to reach the Long Gallery and he went immediately to talk with Dale as he turned back from looking into one of the rooms. As the figure turned round, Burt was confronted by a total stranger.

Max did not waste any time and immediately drew his gun with a silencer attached. Burt saw this coming and he leapt forward, knocking Max to the ground. The two men fought and struggled. Burt was fit and strong despite his age and managed to gain the upper ground but, as he raised his fist to Max, the gun suddenly went off accidentally and Burt crumpled to the floor.

Now Max realized he was in real trouble and started to panic. While he was busy trying to calm himself and plan his next move he heard, above the noise of his loudly beating heart, an uneven thud, thud, not very far away from where he was standing. Unbeknown to Max, the noise was created by Fingers and The Cat moving the heavy wardrobe back to its original position in front of the safe in the master bedroom. Thinking the noise meant that he was about to be discovered he pulled the body of Burt along the corridor back to the Blue Room. There he heaved Burt onto a sofa, landing him in a rather grotesque position, and then spent no more than a few seconds deciding what to do next. If the noise he had heard did mean discovery, then Fingers and The Cat would be caught red-handed and blamed for the shooting. All he had to do was get away as quickly as he could and no one would know that he had been there at all. He remembered to wipe all the doorknobs in the room to remove any fingerprints, but completely forgot in his panic about all the doors he had been opening and closing in the Gallery, and then he was down the rope, burning his hands in the process because of his weight, and back to his car at record speed.

Had Max been not so concerned with the safety of his own skin and turned back while he was scrambling over the perimeter wall to get back to his car, he could have seen Fingers and The Cat coming down the rope, waited for them, taken both of them and the spoils back to Roger and saved himself a lot of explaining.

Finally, The Cat's patience snapped. "For heaven's sake, Fing – stop dreaming about what you are going to do with the sparklers – we aren't out of here yet." Just as he finished speaking, there was the muffled thud of Burt's body dropping to the floor in the Gallery not very far away from them. This noise brought Fingers to his senses and he agreed that they had better get out – fast! Quickly, the two of them pushed the cupboard the last few inches to the wall, stashed all the jewels and the papers in their holdall, gathered their tools together and ran a hasty check of the bedroom to ensure that everything was back in place. They then high-tailed it out of the bedroom and down the Long Gallery to the Blue Room remembering, even in their haste to keep to the left side of the Gallery away from the camera.

As they burst quietly into the Blue Room, their eyes went straight to the balcony. There, outlined by the moonlight, was the grappling hook which held their rope. As they raced towards it The Cat spied Burt's body on the sofa. Grabbing Fingers in full flight, The Cat forced him to turn and survey the twisted body on the sofa. Both of them froze. It occurred to The Cat at first that the person on the sofa was maybe asleep, but as his eyes swept over the figure lying in a position it was almost impossible for a human body to assume voluntarily, he realized that he was looking at an unconscious or dead man. A further quick examination as he reached the sofa found blood on the man's chest and no sign of breathing.

Fingers remained rooted to the spot where he had been stopped, totally unable to understand for a moment what he was looking at. Slowly he realized that this man was dead and he did not like what he saw. Burglary was one thing, but dead bodies gave him the creeps. Who was the man? Why was The Cat examining him so closely? Surely he could see the blood? Finally, he could bear it no longer and launched himself through the french doors and onto the rope. Having decided that there was nothing he could do for the poor unfortunate body, The Cat swiftly followed, knowing that he needed to keep control of Fingers, who would be scared silly and liable to do anything at the bottom of the rope. Fortunately, he had managed to gain on Fingers in the descent and both of them landed on the ground more or less together.

Motioning for Fingers to follow him, The Cat led the way across the grounds, through the Rose Garden and over the wall to their waiting car. Fear kept Fingers from running wild and sensibly he kept up with The Cat all the way to the car, anxious to put as much distance between himself and the body as quickly as possible.

The football game had just finished and the two men were discussing the result. Trying to figure out why the side they supported had lost the game, Stuart Webster, the senior security man, suddenly caught sight of the clock on the wall and the automatic alarm monitor next to it.

"Hey, Dale, it's two minutes past eleven and the alarm system hasn't been set," he said as he looked at the monitor. "What's with Burt?" he mumbled as he got up to go to the operations control room just down the hall.

With Dale on his heels, it didn't take Stuart long to reach the operations room where there was no sign of Burt. Quickly he crossed to the control monitor for the alarm system and noted that the display panel indicated that the Blue Room was 'not ready', which meant only one thing – a door or window was open! Until either the door or window was closed, the alarm could not be set.

"O.K. Dale," said Stuart as he pulled down the switch which controlled the Keep lights, "I'm going up to the Blue Room. You stay here and replace the tape that's in there and keep it so we can look at it again later to see what happened."

Grabbing his cell phone, he almost ran to the Keep and up the stairs to the second floor and the Blue Room. The first thing he saw when he entered the room were the open french doors and the grappling iron embedded in the balcony.

"What the ………?" he thought as he strode through to the balcony and noticed a rope attached to the iron. "Boy, have we got trouble." He knew better than to touch the grappling iron and turned to step back into the room. It was then he saw Burt in an unnaturally contorted position on the sofa.

"Burt!" he cried as he took a couple of strides over to the sofa. Then his professional training took over and, as he placed his fingers on Burt's cold neck to see if there was any sign of a pulse, he visually examined the body noticing the gunshot wound, the blood and no signs of breathing.

"Dale, Burt's dead," said Stuart into his cell phone. "I have closed the door but don't set the alarm - just call the police and get them here as fast as possible," he finished up as he slumped into a chair opposite where Burt lay. He simply couldn't take this in. Who would kill Burt? He doubted that he had an enemy in the world. As he ran over the turn of events in his head, he realized that he and Dale had heard nothing and there had been no indication of any kind of trouble. He could see now that Burt had left his post in the operations room without requesting either himself or Dale to replace him. That was strictly against the rules, so he had no idea why Burt would do such a thing. It was clear that there had been an intruder, but how come the intruder had not shown up on the screen – or had he, and had Burt simply not seen whoever it was?

He had to get down and see Dale, also, he was beginning to feel slightly sick both with emotion and revulsion. How could someone do that to Burt – he never hurt a fly?

By the time he returned to the operations room he could hear the distant sound of the police sirens, thank goodness, and he found Dale fighting back tears.

"Stu, what happened?" cried Dale "did he have a heart attack or a stroke?"

"No," replied Stuart, "I am very much afraid he was murdered."

All the colour drained out of Dale's face. "Murdered!" he said with disbelief. "Murdered?"

"He has been shot," said Stuart. "Somebody has obviously been in the Hall this evening and we didn't know a thing about it. What I can't work out though, is what he was doing up there in the first place. Why didn't he get one of us to go, or at least to monitor the sets while he was gone?"

If Dale was going to come up with some theory in answer to Stuart's remarks, he had no time because the police were arriving.

Detective Superintendent Richardson introduced himself to Stuart and Dale. He was followed by two detective inspectors, a detective sergeant and six uniformed policemen.

"Come with me," said Stuart, "and I will show you where he is."

— The Diamond Talisman —

— Chapter Two —

Kate

Kate was small for her age of nearly fifteen, but what she lacked in stature she made up for in personality and zest for living. She lived with her parents in a cottage on a small estate belonging to an architect who had a busy practice in Manchester, some thirty miles away.

It was indeed an idyllic place in which to live, especially for Kate and her brother James, who had been in this house since they were small children. The big house, where the architect lived, Kate's home and the smaller outbuildings were surrounded by natural gardens which in turn were encircled by rolling meadows with small copses of trees dotted here and there. The woodland, at the back and the west side of the house, followed the gentle slope down to the road and provided a backdrop to the cottage.

Mark and Marianne Foster had accidentally come across the cottage, nestled in a corner of North Wales, when the children were very young, and found that the rent was extremely reasonable because the architect wanted someone living on the estate during his absences at work. The cottage had not been the most up-to-date of buildings, but Mark's 'Do It Yourself' skills and Marianne's flair for design had succeeded in turning it into a warm and loving house which had served as home-base for Kate and James for the past fourteen years.

The cottage and the estate had become the focal point for all their friends who would much rather hang out there in the peace and beauty of the countryside than be standing on street corners in the local village, looking for something to do. As long as the other parents provided transportation for their children, Marianne didn't mind entertaining the whole village if necessary. If the weather was fine, games of Tag, Hide and Seek or Cowboys and Indians beckoned and later the preparation of a barbecue for cooking hot dogs, hamburgers, potatoes and marshmallows kept them all busy until well into the evening.

If rain threatened or actually appeared, then there was Monopoly, Canasta, Pictionary or Scrabble and a host of other games to provide much laughter and entertainment inside. When they were hungry the same outdoor menu was dished up, but this time supervised by Marianne and cooked on the electric stove.

As the childhood years gave way to teens, outdoor pursuits such as walking, hiking and cycling gradually replaced the other games, although not entirely.

The entrance to the estate was through a permanently open gate, permitted to remain that way because of the cattle guard put there to prevent any wandering cows from venturing out on to the road. The driveway meandered up through gently rolling lawns to the main house which had to be bypassed to arrive at Kate's cottage, The Hawthornes, which was situated at the back of the main house.

From the outside The Hawthornes looked like a cottage, but inside it opened out into a good size house with a large kitchen-cum-dining room and a separate living room downstairs and three bedrooms and a bathroom upstairs. In stark contrast to her brother's room, Kate's bedroom was very feminine, decorated throughout in blue and white with accents in the form of daisies with bright yellow centres. As well as her bed and dressing table decked out in the print fabric, Kate had a chair in a blue to match her carpet. The curtains were also in blue, but with a border of daisies along the bottom of the blue fabric. Mark had made a neat corner desk for her on which she could do her homework and higher up on the opposite wall above a chest was her small TV, supported by a wall bracket. It was a room that echoed Kate's outgoing personality and, although Kate was not an overly tidy person, she did her best with her room, much to her mother's relief.

Her favourite time was when she had a friend (usually Amanda, because the two were inseparable) to stay and sleep over. She and Amanda would haul a single mattress out from its storage place under the stairs up to Kate's bedroom, make it up and then the two of them would settle themselves down and never stop talking until sleep got the better of them.

Kate and her friends were at an age where everything to do with the latest fad in the pop world was new and exciting. They would listen to tapes, experiment with ways of wearing their hair and paint their fingernails with light pink, but occasionally with garish coloured nail varnish if they thought they could get away with it! As the tapes played, no matter what state of dress they were in, they would get up and dance to the music, join in the singing or just hum as they tried to work out a new dance. Life was cool.

James, Kate's brother, was now seventeen and had just passed his driving test. He was a typical outdoors buff and was always off to some hiking, rowing or water-skiing event whenever he had time from his schoolwork. He was a strapping lad, just under six feet tall with a dark complexion, twinkling grey/blue eyes and a rugged handsomeness about him. His family was important to James and, even though their common interests were limited, he was very fond of his sister and always kept a wary eye out for her.

Their parents had raised Kate and James very sensibly and both had good, common sense heads on their shoulders. While they had plenty of interests and hobbies, school claimed a good deal of their serious attention. Encouraged by their parents, they saw school as the gateway to a successful future so they worked hard and did well with their studies.

Kate didn't mind schoolwork in spite of the fact that she had to study much more than James to get her good marks. She was very popular at school because of her bubbling personality. It would not be long before her pretty face and model figure would be playing havoc with the opposite sex but Kate remained blissfully unaware of this. Her long, brown hair was the perfect frame for her large brown eyes, upturned nose and small mouth with just a hint of a mischievous grin on it. As yet she had no plans career-wise, except that she liked animals and dancing.

In her spare time, Kate still enjoyed being outside in the fields and woodland that surrounded her own home with her mongrel dog, Lulu. She would sometimes sit on the stump of a felled tree with Lulu by her side, quietly drinking in all the sights and sounds of the countryside. Gradually her gaze would wander to the sky above, looking at the shapes of the clouds and wondering what the future held in store for her. She never got an answer, of course, but occasionally a feeling of disquiet descended on her that she could not define specifically, no matter how hard she tried. The sensation wasn't good, but it certainly wasn't bad and it defied any further description except a vague suggestion that it was perhaps something connected to the future. She knew that there was nothing in her past that would produce this unsettling feeling. She wished the notion would become clearer but it didn't and it really was not enough to cause her continued worry. Still, it was odd, and she found herself wishing more and more that she could see into the future but, as her mother had once said, being able to see the future would spoil what was to come!

Deciding such thoughts could wait until another time, Kate would usually tuck them into the back of her mind, call Lulu, and continue her walk. Indeed, the thoughts would not surface again until the next time she sat on that same stump and looked at the sky and clouds.

Her best friend, Amanda, was quite a bit taller and more heavily built than Kate. She was an attractive girl too but she was inclined to be quieter and didn't have the self-confidence that Kate had, which made her less out-going than her friend. This was perhaps due to the fact that she was an only child and did not have the wide circle of friends that Kate and James enjoyed. Amanda and her family lived in a small village about two miles from Kate's house and she also had been blessed with sensible parents and a secure home life. Like Kate, she was crazy about the local teen discos (when their parents would let them go), and all kinds of animals.

It was a hot Wednesday in July just after the start of the school holidays when Kate and Amanda found themselves at a loose end. Kate's mother unexpectedly came to the rescue. She needed to go on a shopping trip to Chester and she suggested that the girls might like to go to Chester Zoo. She could drop them there and return to pick them up in about three to three and a half hours. The girls jumped at this idea because Chester Zoo was one of the most attractive and popular Zoological Gardens in the country. Kate and Amanda loved to visit but because of the distance they didn't get there often so they needed no second bidding. Marianne dropped them off at eleven o'clock in the morning with a promise to be back between two and half-past two to collect them.

Dr. Lloyd, the police surgeon, had arrived only a few minutes after Detective Superintendent Richardson. He passed three police officers working to secure the scene of the crime so that nothing could be moved and the scene would remain preserved, just as it was when the body was discovered. After a cursory examination of the body it was revealed that Burt had indeed been shot and, as far as Dr. Lloyd could ascertain, this had happened probably two or three hours ago.

"Anything interesting?" asked John Richardson.

"No, it all looks fairly straightforward," replied Dr. Lloyd. "However, the body has been moved – he certainly wasn't shot on this sofa. It could have happened outside this room and the body maybe was dragged or carried to this sofa and just left in this rather unnatural position."

"Right," replied Detective Superintendent Richardson, "we will carry out a careful search. Anything else you can tell us at the moment?"

"No, not yet. We'll just have to wait until the autopsy is done – I'll see what I can do about getting the preliminary results to you later today. I'll be in touch as soon as I have anything."

The doctor said he would sign the death certificate after the autopsy, decreed that the body could be removed to the morgue when the police were ready, and left.

Following the departure of the police surgeon, the police officers returned and started to investigate and photograph various aspects of the crime scene, which included not only the room but the balcony to which was attached the grappling iron and the rope, and the adjacent Long Gallery. Other back- up police officers arrived and dispersed to search the Keep for any sign of breaking and entering that would support the possibility that the murder could have happened because of a burglary. They were looking not only for evidence of breaking and entering, but for more subtle evidence like clothing fibres, hair strands and blood samples, plus any other strange looking substances or objects.

While his men were busy dusting for latent prints, Detective Superintendent Richardson went downstairs with Detective Inspector Barry Bradford. As they walked down the ornate carved staircase, a look of more than concern showed on the face of John Richardson and Barry Bradford knew better than to interrupt him.

Detective Superintendent Richardson was a tall man in his late thirties with kindly brown eyes deeply set in a squarish, determined looking face, surrounded by a shock of almost black hair – still! He was known as a stickler for detail and 'hunches', which had invariably produced results. His superior officer did not always agree with these hunches, but he had learned better than to question Richardson too closely. He now accepted that any inkling or gut feeling on the part of John Richardson was a serious consideration. He was not the first person who had combined this uncanny perception with standard police investigative procedures, but unlike one or two other officers the Chief Inspector had known who had also acted on 'gut feelings', Richardson was never wrong. It was a 'hunch' about this case preying on John Richardson's mind as he walked downstairs.

Barry Bradford had worked for three years with Detective Superintendent Richardson. He admired him, respected him and had, like D.I. Jones, very quickly learned to read him. Barry was nearly as tall as his boss, slightly heavier and a very friendly and outgoing person. He was not only invaluable to his boss, but was often the one who smoothed troubled waters.

"Stuart," said Detective Superintendent Richardson as he entered the control room, "this is Detective Inspector Barry Bradford." Pausing only to allow the two men to shake hands, he went on, "Perhaps Dale could take the Detective Inspector down to the Gun Room. I don't think the Marquess has the same type of weapon that killed Burt, but we must check."

"No problem," replied Stuart, nodding at Dale to go with D.I. Bradford to the Gun Room which was one floor below them. As they entered the Gun Room, D.I. Bradford was impressed with what appeared to be an arsenal of guns. On closer inspection they were mostly of historical value only, or rifles and shotguns for hunting. Apart from a few ancient muzzle-loading flintlocks, there was no sign of any small hand weapons.

In the meantime, Detective Superintendent Richardson was quizzing Stuart about his activities from the time they had switched off the football match on television.

"Are you absolutely sure that you didn't touch anything?" Detective Superintendent Richardson asked Stuart.

"Well, I did put my fingers on his neck to check for a pulse," admitted Stuart, "but apart from that, nothing. I noticed the grappling iron and the rope but I didn't touch either of them."

"And you had no indication of anything happening in the house, prior to the time you found that the alarm had not been set – you didn't hear anything?" continued Detective Superintendent Richardson.

"Not a thing," confirmed Stuart. "But to tell you the truth, what I cannot understand was why Burt was up there in the first place and why he left his post without asking one of us to cover. It was so out of character for him."

"Apart from the vault which is in the control room, do you know if there is any other place of safekeeping for papers or jewellery in the house?" enquired Detective Superintendent Richardson.

At that moment D.I. Bradford and Dale returned from the Gun Room and Dale went over to slot in the video tape that had been in use at the time of the murder. He started to rewind it and then fast forward it to the point just before he and Stuart went off duty.

"No," replied Stuart, "everything is kept in the vault, including her Ladyship's jewels, so I have no idea what anyone might be looking for upstairs, if it was a robbery. There are, of course, plenty of valuable pictures and furniture, but nothing is missing as far as I can see. I will double-check my inventory list though, first thing in the morning."

"Aha!" exclaimed Stuart as Dale found the right spot on the video. "So there was somebody up there!" A back view of Max appeared on the screen and Stuart did a double take. "Dale, whoever it was, he looks exactly like you from the back."

"Yes, I suppose he does, although I'm not too sure how I look from behind," replied Dale with a slightly nervous laugh.

The four men watched intently as the video continued to show Max trying the doors. Then Burt arrived and from what they could see of him, he didn't look at all concerned or worried.

"Hey, maybe he did think it was me up there." suggested Dale.

"It does look likely," Detective Superintendent Richardson said, "but now look what's happening!"

The camera had recorded the fight between Burt and Max, but the lack of sound made it look a little disjointed, like a silent movie. They saw the gun appear in Max's hand, Burt crumple to the floor, and Max, but not full face, struggle to stand up. The camera then recorded Max dragging Burt towards the Blue Room, and then there was nothing on the tape except the empty Gallery until Dale had switched it off to keep it for the police.

"That's going to be very helpful," said Detective Superintendent Richardson. "I'll take this tape with me. Our experts will certainly be able to enhance the picture so they we can pick up more details from close-ups."

At that moment Detective Superintendent Richardson was summoned by his other Detective Inspector, Jim Jones, and with D.I. Bradford, excused himself and returned to the Long Gallery.

"Well, what have you found?" he enquired as he entered the Long Gallery.

"There are spots of blood over here on the carpet, and on the wooden floor." said Jim Jones. "Also, by the look of the nap of this carpet, a scuffle could have taken place out here, and then perhaps the body was dragged into the Blue Room," he continued.

"Good work," said Detective Superintendent Richardson, as he explained briefly what he had seen on the video downstairs. "We saw on the video that whoever it was who killed Burt certainly wasn't wearing gloves, so I think dusting for fingerprints on all the doors on the right hand side of the Gallery might produce some interesting results. And we'd better go over the Long Gallery with a fine-tooth comb. Maybe we'll find more evidence to tell us what he was here for."

Detective Sergeant George Green volunteered the information that there was absolutely no evidence of any breaking and entering in any other room in the Keep so far, and if that was the case, it seemed odd that the murder had taken place, unless Burt happened to be the target.

"I somehow doubt that," mused Detective Superintendent Richardson. "From the video it does look as though Burt could have mistaken the intruder for Dale, and both Stuart and Dale had nothing but praise for Burt and the way he worked. Given that, I cannot see that he was on any kind of hit list!"

"Hey, Sir," said Jim again with some excitement in his voice, "we've just found some prints on the handle of this first door we've dusted, so at least we have a chance of finding out who our mystery intruder is. I don't like to think that whoever killed Burt Manley might get away with it."

"Well, there was definitely a stranger in the house," concluded Detective Superintendent Richardson, "but at the moment it looks as though his target was Burt, in the absence of any evidence of a robbery. But why?" He paused for a moment, looking puzzled, then said, "Well, I'm going to get back to the station. We'll find out where Lord and Lady Ryerdale are on holiday and let them know what's happened. At the same time I'll double-check with them that there are no other safes or vaults in the Hall which may contain valuables that no one has been told about."

It was turning out to be a sweltering day and Kate and Amanda began to feel hot and sticky as they wandered around looking at all the different animals, each kind in their own enclosure, landscaped to match as closely as possible the animal's native background. The girls laughed with delight as they watched the cocky penguins strutting up and down with their peculiar waddle and then diving into the water to swim with grace and beauty. They managed to be on time to see the sea lions being fed with fish from a bucket by their keeper. They also spent a long time looking at the elephants although the elephants now had such a big new enclosure you could hardly see some of them. There were still the odd ones, though, who had decided it was their duty to entertain their admirers and they put on quite a display of trying to squirt water with their trunks over the fence and security ditch at the visitors.

"Oh, let's sit down for a while and have an ice cream," said Amanda as they neared the Ostrich pen, as she had seen an ice-cream cart just outside the fence.

"Good idea," agreed Kate. "You get them and I'll bag this seat over here."

Having bought two very large ice creams, the girls settled down on the seat to enjoy them. Not too far away there was another seat on which sat two men talking to a third who had a foot on the end of the bench and was leaning towards them, talking excitedly.

"Mandy," said Kate, "see that ostrich over there standing by himself – he is quite different from the rest of them. Look, he's a lovely golden colour instead of dark brown and black and he's got such an elegant neck. And look at those huge soft brown eyes!"

"I wonder why he is so different," replied Amanda. "He's even smaller than the rest and he isn't standing with them – look, he's by himself. Do you know something, Kate, I think he is looking at us." The two girls were curious and even more so because they noticed that the people who passed the enclosure didn't seem to notice the difference in the colour and size of the ostrich they were looking at compared to the plain black, brown and white of the rest of the birds.

As they sat there in silence enjoying their ice creams and studying the golden ostrich, bits and pieces of the conversation between the men on the next bench were reaching their ears. At first the girls did not take much notice but it gradually dawned on them that this was not a normal conversation.

In fact, sitting on the bench near to them were none other than Fingers and The Cat. Instead of the streamlined and rather odd image they presented in the leotards, hoods and tight-fitting gloves they wore when working, they were now dressed in jeans and sports shirts just like a couple of tourists enjoying a day out at the zoo. However, their presence had nothing whatsoever to do with any interest in the zoo. It was simply a convenience. They knew that in such an open place with so many children about, they would be unlikely to be seen by anyone they knew or who knew them. Some of the characters they mixed with in their line of work probably wouldn't even know what a zoo was! The last thing they wanted was for Roger Corr to know where they were.

This meeting was with their fence, Freddie Bendell, who was negotiating with third parties interested in buying what Fingers and The Cat had on offer after their visit to Ryerdale Hall. This was work that Freddie really enjoyed. Not for him the dangers of robbery and murder – there were better ways to make money! He would get a very substantial cut from all of this, provided he could keep Fingers on an even keel and persuade The Cat to do what was best for all three of them. Also dressed in jeans and sports shirt, which covered several tattoos, Freddie was quite a handsome guy. Moderately tall, he had a golden tan and an enviable, muscular build. His face was like granite – he never gave anything away and his blue eyes were cold and steely enough to stare down any negotiator. He was good at what he did and charged a lot for doing it, but Fingers and The Cat were prepared to pay for the best. They wanted to deal with Freddie because he was the one fence they knew who had never done business with Roger Corr.

Looking back, the pair of them couldn't believe that they had pulled the job off so successfully. Roger was bound to be hunting for them by now, but once the arrangements for the disposal of the diamond and the other jewellery were made and the money was in their hands, they would be out of the country, quite confident that Corr would not find them.

"… and this man was on the sofa – all horribly twisted," said Fingers, "horrible it was – dead bodies make me feel all creepy!"

"Oh shut up, Fingers," said Freddie, leaning further over the end of the bench towards Fingers and prodding his shoulder. "We've heard all that before and there's nothing we can do about it. Besides, he'll have been found and the matter reported to the police by now. Look at it this way, the police will be so busy trying to find out what happened to him that they may not be too careful in looking for evidence of a robbery."

"I suppose so, I never thought of that," said Fingers.

"Well think about it now," said Freddie. "Now, back to the sparklers. I've got somebody interested and he'll give about eight million, if that catches your fancy?"

"Not so fast, Freddie," interrupted a serious and thoughtful Cat. "There's much more at stake here. The whole heist is worth ten times that amount."

"Oh yes," replied Freddie, "and how do you think you're going to get rid of the Mirendah? Word of a diamond that size is bound to spread like wildfire and make it too hot to handle."

The Cat looked at him with a smirk creeping over his face. "That may be so, but there's not been any talk about it in recent years and after it has been polished and cut, no one is going to know where it came from, and as for the Bearer Bonds we ..."

Suddenly the men went into more of a huddle and the girls could no longer hear what they were saying, although they were desperately trying.

"Oh Kate, that's awful," whispered Amanda, all colour draining from her face as she looked at her friend.

Kate, forever the practical one, said quietly, "Listen, Amanda, I think it would be a good idea if you went to look for one of the zoo security guards. We have to report this." Both of them seemed totally unaware of the danger they had put themselves in by overhearing the conversation.

"O.K.," replied Amanda. "Will you be alright here? You won't move, will you?"

"Oh, don't be daft," whispered Kate. "I am quite happy to watch the ostrich, and I'll also keep my ears open for anything that might tell us where the murder took place. If the men move I will try and follow them. I'll keep an eye open for you coming back at the same time, but you must hurry!" She grinned to encourage her friend, who looked anything but happy about the situation.

After Amanda had gone rather reluctantly, Kate went on watching the golden ostrich. He was still standing on his own, a good way from the rest of the birds and looking directly at her. Kate really didn't know why the bird was studying her, but he was, with a gentle, piercing stare. At the same time, she was also keeping her ears open, hoping to catch some more scraps of conversation coming from the nearby bench. The three men seemed to be furiously talking, but she could not hear what they were saying because they had huddled together and faced away from her so the sound of their voices was being carried the other way.

As Kate watched the ostrich it slowly made its way over to the fence that enclosed the compound. Forgetting all about the men on the bench, she found herself getting up from the seat and being irresistibly drawn towards the fence which formed a barrier between the public and the enclosure. Kate was completely mesmerized by the ostrich's big brown eyes and she felt rooted to the spot, quite incapable of moving.

— The Diamond Talisman —

— Chapter Three —

Friends And Foes

Oscar was the name of the ostrich that so fascinated Kate and Amanda, but it would be a while before Kate discovered his name. Like many other bigger birds, ostriches have a certain regal air about them. On the other hand, you would discover a less regal side to them should you come too close and find their tendency to peck and lash out with the big, sharp claws on their feet! The normal black and white plumage which covers their body had been much in demand at one time for ladies' fans and head-dresses, but with modern dress, that demand has passed into history. They are the kind of bird that if you look at them once, they may appear ungainly and ugly, but if you look again, they can be streamlined and handsome. It depends on the mood of the onlooker.

Oscar was clearly different. He really was a most attractive and unusual ostrich. He was slightly smaller than the other birds and instead of the familiar black and white feathers that are seen on the male ostrich, Oscar's plumage was almost golden – a beautiful dark bronze gold. His shimmering loose-textured wing and tail feathers were silver rather than white with a silky texture. Oscar's neck and legs were covered with a brilliant silver white down. Around his head this down almost looked like a halo, which made the perfect frame for his huge amber eyes.

As well as being smaller than the other birds, whose height generally reached about eight feet, he had a longer, more streamlined body than the rest of the ostriches in the enclosure. The average ostrich can weigh up to 400 pounds, but Oscar looked as though he would not be much more than 350 pounds.

Like all ostriches Oscar's feet had two toes only, one large and one small with the large one bearing the full weight of the bird and it had a wicked looking claw at the end of it. If threatened or annoyed, the ostrich can do considerable damage to its victim with that claw.

It could be said that Oscar had been in Chester Zoo for the past six months. Before that, it could be said, Oscar had been in safari parks and zoos around the world, on the plains of Africa and in the realms of historic time. Oscar was sometimes in these places and sometimes he was not in these places. He was in zoos and safari parks because that is where people expected to find an ostrich, but if he had a job to do he would come and go as he pleased. Keepers and attendants were never really aware of his presence or absence and Oscar made sure that remained the case. It would never have done for a mere mortal to become suspicious of his movements!

Oscar had, in fact, been around since the beginning of time. He came from the wonderful Kingdom of Light, the dwelling place of angels and saints; he was no less than an emissary of God. He looked like an ostrich, he acted like an ostrich and he mixed with other ostriches, but his mission down the ages had been to help and defend people who could not be helped or defended by anyone on Earth. Being a bird, he could not talk or make any conversation but he had the power to transfer his thoughts to other animals from the Kingdom of Light and also to humans when he chose so to do.

Oscar's home, the Kingdom of Light, was a place of such beauty and joy that it was indescribable. It was a place Oscar preferred not to leave but he had to on many, many occasions. As with his fellow secret agents, Oscar worked on Earth most of the time, because God had chosen His angels to mix with the minds, hearts and bodies of people living anywhere on Earth who needed to be re-assured or guided by God's love for them.

In addition to the abundance of love he had for each and every one of the people he was called to protect, Oscar's task was to ensure that no harm would come to them and that ultimately they would know that they were safe under the protective wing of God's love and need never be afraid.

Even though he had supernatural powers and could do anything he wanted to do, Oscar often found it incredibly difficult to co-exist with ostriches on Earth. Their behaviour was the exact opposite of what he was used to and he had to struggle sometimes to remember what life was like for him when he lived as an ordinary ostrich on Earth, before he became a secret agent.

Unfortunately, although he tried to mix freely and make friends with the other ostriches in the zoo his difference in size and colour made this difficult for him. Most of the time the other birds, who were a little bit suspicious of him, just ignored him but sometimes they bullied him, pecking at him and flapping their useless wings. Although he was used to this teasing and taunting after such a long time, Oscar could never really accept this. He was, after all, an ostrich and he longed to have other ostrich friends, so it made him very sad that none of the other birds, wherever he had been, wanted to have much to do with him. Occasionally, down through the ages he had managed to make the casual ostrich friend, but most of the time he was a lonely bird. However, the countless number of times he was able to help people made up for the rather friendless existence he led.

Oscar had developed his own way of dealing with bullying. If, after trying to be friendly with each new bird, his advances were met with distrust or hostility from the other bird, he would keep himself to himself. As well as telling himself that there was nothing wrong with him and that it was the other birds that had the problem because they didn't even try to get to know him, he knew that he could disappear completely if the going got too bad. Most of the time he was a solitary figure at the zoos or parks but he knew that he was at Chester Zoo for a specific reason. At this time he just had to be patient and wait for the current reason to make itself known as he knew it would.

To while away the time during which the other birds chose to ignore him completely, Oscar would think about two very old friends of his, both, like him, special emissaries from the Kingdom of Light. One was a Bald Eagle called Isia, who spent most of his time in Canada and the other was Jenza, a Siberian Tiger who resided primarily in the mountain woodlands and high cliffs of South East Russia. Jenza was much larger than other tigers, with paler fur – light orange instead of dark orange – and with brown stripes rather than black. He had a luxuriant coat, which grew to an extra length to keep him warm in the winter. He had longer hair than other tigers on his cheeks and smoldering eyes, much like those of his distant cousin, the domestic cat.

Jenza spent most of his time waiting for calls from other emissaries around the world who needed his help. He did not usually work on a one-to-one basis with people needing help or protection because they could be quite frightened of him, but he was there as a back-up when needed, which was on a fairly regular basis. He had worked with Oscar on many occasions when he was needed to scare someone into submission or to stop them using weapons. Oscar, Jenza and Isia also enjoyed one another's company off duty whenever possible.

Isia, the Bald Eagle lived far away from Oscar and Jenza on the Pacific coast of Western Canada amongst rivers, lakes, forests and mountains. The Bald Eagle is so named because of the white feathers on its head and neck in startling contrast to the black feathers covering the rest of its body. Like Oscar, Isia acts as a personal emissary when needed but also, like Jenza, can be a support to other emissaries. Isia, Oscar and Jenza go back a long way and, when they are working together, it is very easy for them to anticipate what the other is going to do. They all have extra-sensory perception, which allows them to be on the same wavelength. When all three of them are working on the same mission, they automatically know what the others are doing and this means that each can concentrate more fully on their individual tasks. These abilities result in terrific teamwork. It has never failed and will always be so.

On this hot Wednesday afternoon Oscar sees, at long last, the human he has been designated to look after and protect. Her name is Kate and Oscar knows, without a shadow of a doubt, that his lonely days at the zoo have come to an end because Kate is going to need him. The first problem facing him is how to get Kate's attention, which he must do before he can begin to think of getting out of the ostrich compound. Even though he could free himself from the zoo at a moment's notice, he cannot do this until the person he is there to help accepts that he is a special ostrich and outwardly bonds with him.

Having seen Amanda leave, Oscar feels that now is his opportunity, especially since Kate has been looking at him again. The ostriches had recently been fed and while the other birds were pecking through the food the keeper had left for them, Oscar took himself, unnoticed, over to the fencing which surrounded the compound. Of course, there were the inner and the outer fences, but that did not deter him. He watched Kate get up and come over to have another look at him and he moved to stand directly in front of her and fixed her with the most riveting, but gentle, look. Kate was transfixed. She had never before seen an ostrich like him and those eyes seemed really special. She fell in love with him.

Before she realized what was happening, the ostrich vanished right before her eyes. She looked around for him, frantically, but he was nowhere to be seen. Puzzled and disappointed, she started to walk back to the bench thrusting her hands into the big pockets of her long shirt. She was startled when she felt a ball of soft feathers in her right pocket and, pulling it out, saw a miniature ostrich cradled in her palm looking exactly the same as he had in his full size. Kate sat down on the bench, not believing what she was seeing and unable to understand how it could have happened. It was nonsense! A minute ago there had been a fully-grown, enormous bird on the other side of two fences and now he had been transformed into a miniature bird in her pocket. Not only was she completely mystified; she couldn't think what to do with the bundle of feathers in her hand.

She did not have time to give this much thought because while all her attention was been taken up with the ostrich she had failed to notice the three men on the next bench seat get up and saunter over to where she sat.

"Well, well, well. What do we have here?" enquired Freddie, as he neared Kate's bench.

Hearing his voice, Kate's fingers seemed to automatically curl over the ostrich in her hand and she casually slipped him back into her shirt pocket just as the men arrived at her bench. Suddenly, Kate was worried. Why are they here, she wondered, and why are they talking to me? Did they see the ostrich? She began to feel really scared as two of the men sat down, one on either side of her.

"So, you've been sitting here for quite a while?" asked The Cat, not waiting for a reply because he had known exactly how long she had been there.

"It's hot," said Kate, with a sickly feeling in her stomach, "so I decided to sit for a while." It was a pretty lame excuse but it was the best she could think of at that moment.

"Yes, well we think it has been just a bit too long," countered Freddie, reaching for her wrist and grasping it in a grip of iron. "If you know what's good for you, m'dear, you'll come along with us – no messing!"

Kate lost all the confidence she had felt when she sent Amanda to find a security guard and started to struggle. "Let go of me!" she yelled, "I'm not going anywhere with you. If you don't …."

At that point, shielded by his two friends, Freddie clamped a large hand over her mouth and physically dragged Kate to her feet. "Now, I'm going to take my hand away from your mouth and if there's one more word out of you then I shall have to deal with you and it won't be very nice," Freddie softly hissed at her. "Now, start walking."

Suddenly Kate felt what she thought was the muzzle of a gun in the small of her back and decided she had no choice but to walk and keep her mouth closed. There were other people about but not many because the penguins were about to be fed and most of the people had left the area around the ostrich enclosure. She dared not call out because of Freddie's threat and she was also worried about the ostrich in her pocket. She realized with a sense of relief that they had not seen the bird as she had pocketed him just as Freddie and The Cat had approached her.

She had to walk very quickly to keep up with them and she bit her lip hard so that they could not see that she was on the verge of tears. Hemming her in, the men reached the exit in about four minutes where they hustled Kate out of the exit gate and into the car park. Trying to look as relaxed as possible, to avoid any curious looks or glances from passers-by, they half pushed and half dragged Kate to where their car was parked. Both Freddie and The Cat realized that the girl who had been sitting with Kate must also have heard what they had been talking about. Unfortunately for them, they could not have prevented her departure. Even if they had attempted to stop her, it would have been difficult because of the number of people about at that particular time and two kidnapped girls would have proved more difficult to handle than one. So they had let Amanda go, not quite knowing how much she had overheard, but decided to take Kate with them as a security measure against any trouble Amanda might cause them.

They knew nothing about Oscar. They had seen Kate get up and go over to the enclosure to have a closer look at the birds as they kept a wary eye on her, ready to pounce at the slightest sign that she might move on. But no, she returned to sit on the bench and then they decided to act swiftly and simply did not see the miniature Oscar being put into her pocket. Little did they know that they were carrying Oscar along with Kate and that he would ultimately create untold difficulties for them.

"Hello, is that Lord Ryerdale?" enquired Detective Superintendent Richardson.

"Yes, this is Ryerdale," replied the slightly curt voice on the other end of the line. It was, after all, only half past six in the morning and Lord Ryerdale was not expecting a telephone call at that early time of day.

"Your Lordship, this is Detective Superintendent Richardson from Chester Police Headquarters. I am afraid I have some rather sad and alarming news for you."

"Oh, what's the problem?" enquired Lord Ryerdale, slightly concerned that the call was from the police.

John Richardson went on to explain all that had happened at Ryerdale Hall and when he had finished there was silence on the other end of the telephone.

"Are you still there, Sir?" asked the detective.

"I'm still here," replied Lord Ryerdale with a heavy sadness in his voice. "Poor Burt, he has been with us for a long time – does his family know?"

"Yes, Stuart Webster went with one of my officers and told them last night," continued Detective Superintendent

Richardson. "Of course, he will not have given them all the details. I will be going to see them shortly and will explain how it happened."

"Thank you, Detective Superintendent. I just can't believe it – have you any idea why it happened?" enquired Lord Ryerdale.

"Not at this moment, but we are working on it," replied the Detective Superintendent. "Apart from having to tell you the sad news, My Lord, I was hoping that you would be able to tell me if there is any place in the Hall where you keep valuables, other than in the vault. At the moment it is unlikely that any kind of robbery took place as there would not appear to be anything missing, but sometimes robbery is the motive for murder and we cannot overlook the possibility."

"Well, as a matter of fact, yes," conceded Lord Ryerdale, somewhat embarrassed that he had never shared the existence and location of his own personal safe with the police before now. The reason for this was two-fold. First of all, he had not wanted anyone to know that he possessed The Mirendah Diamond because that would have been an open invitation for theft. Secondly, there were the old guilty feelings about his family harbouring stolen property, even though the theft took place over one hundred years ago. "But I thought you said there was no burglary?"

"Not as far as we can ascertain at the moment, sir. No, as I said, there is no evidence of that. We just wanted to double check with you in case there was somewhere else we had failed to look," said Detective Superintendent Richardson. "Can you tell me where the safe is?"

"Yes, I can but you will not be able to open it because of the combination." Suddenly making a snap decision, Lord Ryerdale continued, "I will make arrangements to fly home today. I need to be there for Burt's family, and when I arrive home we can look through the safe. I would be very surprised if anyone had found it, let alone managed to get into it!"

"Fine, Sir. Is there anything else I can do for you before then?" enquired Detective Superintendent Richardson.

"Yes," replied Lord Ryerdale, "perhaps you would call the Hall and tell them that I will be returning today and I will be in touch with Hayton, my chauffeur, when I have the flight times sorted out. Goodbye for now, Richardson, and thank you for calling."

"You can be sure I will ring the Hall. Goodbye," replied the Detective Superintendent. Replacing the receiver, he was relieved that Lord Ryerdale was coming home, although he was somewhat annoyed that he had not seen fit to tell the police or any of his staff about this extra safe. The association between Ryerdale Hall and the local police detachment went back a long way and John Richardson had assumed that he had the complete trust of the Marquess.

After replacing the receiver at his end, Lord Ryerdale rose and started to pace the floor. His aristocratic bearing was obvious but with that any other traditional comparison ended. Andrew, Lord Ryerdale, was first and foremost a business man and worked hard at being extremely successful and helping other people. The result of this combination resulted in little free time and tremendous responsibilities.

Well into his forties, he was just under six feet tall with a good muscular build, thanks in no small part to his fitness commitment. He looked tanned and healthy with a mop of curly black/grey hair. Even after three weeks in the sun, his face was still etched with lines indicating stress and effort. It was not easy juggling all his enterprises, even with expert help and he rarely had time for relaxation.

In spite of his success and affluence, he had a tendency to be sensitive and overly protective towards his family, both past and present, and the Ryerdale name. At that moment he pondered a little on the history of The Mirendah Diamond and tried to work out why he felt so guilty every time he had to deal with it.

In 1867, Lord Cecil Ryerdale, heir to the Marquess of Ryerdale, had held an important position in a large company engaged by the builders of the Suez Canal. His work meant frequent travel between England and the headquarters of the Anglo-French Suez Canal Company in Ismailia. Cecil lived in the same style in the Middle East as he did in Wales. He mixed with the best of society, including crowned heads and prominent politicians when visiting Cairo. In Ismailia, he mingled with his corporate associates, including Arab businessmen, who always had their ears to the ground for any possible deals, shady or otherwise. Ismailia was at a crossroads for illegal trading and consequently there was always underworld information that could easily be bought.

The problem with Cecil Ryerdale was that, although he had more money than he could possibly know what to do with, he always wanted more. This element of greed in his character became the driving force in his life and he was always on the look out for some kind of deal which would increase his wealth.

On one of his many trips, he heard about the fabulous diamond called The Mirendah. The Sultan of Mirendah whose palace was in Karbala near Baghdad, owned the stone. When Cecil first learned about the diamond, he tucked the information away in the back of his mind but considered the possibility of its acquisition. Gradually, his desire to possess the stone worked its way into becoming an obsession and he couldn't believe his luck when he heard that the diamond was going to be returned by the Sultan to a Maharaja in India, the country of the stone's origin.

Elaborate plans were made for the transportation of the diamond. It would leave Karbala on a camel train that would carry the stone to the Indian border. Just beyond the border, the stone would be transferred to a railway train to make the journey to its final destination in Jaipur.

Cecil, of course, had his strategically deployed spies bring him a detailed account of the journey and this formed the foundation for his own plot to steal the precious cargo en route. After giving the matter careful thought, he felt it best if the theft took place just inside the Indian border. This would supply a red herring for the investigators and draw their attention away from the Middle East. To support his plans and through his various contacts, Cecil was able to organize the theft to be carried out by Indians which further gave credence to the diversion.

The train robbery was carried out with daring and precision by the most experienced criminals that Cecil could hire. It was pulled off without a hitch, all his hired men were paid off handsomely and Cecil returned with The Mirandeh to Wales. Authorities in India and then the Middle East launched a thorough investigation but they never did find out either who carried out the robbery or who was the mastermind.

After returning to Britain for good in 1871, Lord Ryerdale settled down at the family home in Wales to resume his duties as heir to the Marquesate. In 1875, his father died and Cecil succeeded to the title, which he held only for a year and two months, as he himself was killed in a hunting accident on the estate. The diamond remained in his hidden safe and Cecil had the only key, which he kept in the back of a drawer in his desk. He told no one about the diamond and savoured the fact that it was his.

Cecil had been married, but had no children, so when he died his younger brother Walter succeeded to the title. When Walter took over Cecil's study he carefully, or so he thought, cleared out the desk, but the small key to the safe was tucked away in a corner and was not discovered. It wasn't until ten years later, during a search for a lost document, that Walter discovered the key. Even though it had been some years after Cecil had died, Walter, knowing his older brother, knew that the key definitely belonged to some lock and he intended to find out where that lock was. He searched the Hall from top to bottom but found nothing until the following spring, when all the carpets were removed from the private apartments for their annual cleaning. Walter came into his study to spend the morning at work and on his way over to his desk he heard one of the floorboards creak. He retraced his steps because he thought this noise might be evidence of some kind of rot in the wooden flooring.

What he found on closer inspection, was a small, loose piece in one of the floorboards. He was able to put his fingernails under one end of the board and gently raise it up. Instead of it all falling apart from rot as he thought it might, it revealed a small cavity in the floor, no bigger than twelve inches by nine inches and in the cavity was a small box. Walter knew instinctively that the key he had found in his desk would fit the lock on this box and he wasted no time in testing his theory, retrieving the key and opening the box. Inside was something wrapped in paper and when he opened it up he dropped into his chair in a state of shock as he recognized The Mirendah Diamond. He had, of course, read all the news at the time about the theft of the diamond from the train and he had known Cecil's greed well enough to know why The Mirendah was underneath the floorboard. What he did not know was what he was going to do with the Diamond.

He turned this problem around and around in his head for the next few weeks, but in the end he decided to keep the diamond under lock and key and never admit to anyone outside the family that he had it. He knew it was rather a cowardly way out, but he did not want to admit that his brother had been a first-class thief and face the scandal that would almost certainly follow when the news got out.

So the diamond was returned to safekeeping under the floorboard for a number of years with an outline of its history being passed along to each succeeding Marquess of Ryerdale. Then William, father of Andrew, the present Marquess, decided that it would be safer to keep it in a hidden safe built into the wall of the master bedroom. It had remained there ever since.

— Chapter Four —

The Depths of Despair

When the rather odd-looking quartet of Kate, Freddie, Fingers and The Cat arrived at the place where Freddie had parked his car, Oscar, hidden unseen in Kate's pocket, was wondering if there was anything he could do at this stage to help. He knew only too well that the men had no idea that he was there, which was to his advantage. It would have been possible for him to come out of Kate's pocket, rise to his full height and use his claws and beak to attack the culprits, which he would have been quite happy to do, but he knew this would not be a sensible move. There were three of them and only one of him. Two men would not have been a problem, but the third, especially with a pistol, could have meant Kate losing him right at the start of her troubles, before he even had a chance to establish a bond with her and gain her trust. Although he knew the type of girl she was, what she liked and what she didn't like and how she lived her life, it was too early for him to know how she would react if he were to launch an attack. Besides, there was the remote possibility that he might get caught which would defeat the whole purpose of being there for Kate. No, he decided, he could not take the risk.

Freddie meanwhile had unlocked the front and back door of the car and Kate was roughly pushed into the back seat. The Cat clambered in after her and Fingers went round to sit in front with Freddie. They sped off as fast as they dared without arousing suspicion towards their temporary lodgings in the village of Chilfray, where Freddie had rented a small house at the end of a cul-de-sac on the outskirts of the village.

Kate was looking very uncomfortable in the back seat and The Cat felt a bit sorry for her.

"Now listen to me," said The Cat as they drove towards Chilfray, "as long as you behave yourself and do as you are told, nothing will happen to you, but if you start to give us problems, then you'll be in deep trouble – understood?"

Kate was so scared that it took her all her time to mutter "yes," which seemed to satisfy The Cat, as he fell silent again and they continued their journey.

Kate began to wonder if they would ever get to where they were going – it seemed a long time since they started out from the zoo. They didn't blindfold her, but she did not recognize any of the places they passed, probably because she was scared of what might happen to her. She was so frightened, she had even forgotten about the ostrich in her pocket, and it wasn't until she felt a small but definite scratch on her leg, that she was reminded of him. For a moment she thought again about all the bizarre events leading up to this situation and this totally strange bird that had suddenly shrunk from a full sized ostrich to a bundle of feathers, now in her pocket, and found that his little scratch was quite comforting. She felt that no matter how strange the ostrich was, he was her friend and that helped her feel a little calmer.

Finally they arrived at their destination and Kate was pulled out of the car. When she was on her feet, she put her hand into her pocket and around the bird, to protect him from anything that might squash him. She was hustled in through the front door of what seemed to be a very ordinary house. She was led into a stuffy and very warm room and ordered by The Cat to sit on a straight-backed chair. Quickly, Fingers tied her hands and her feet to the chair while Freddie announced that they were going out to get something to eat.

"When we come back," he said, almost rubbing his hands together in glee, "we'll have a little discussion about what you heard while you were sitting on that bench at the zoo."

With that the three of them left, banging both the door of the room where Kate was tied up and the front door behind them and Kate was alone. Now that she could cry the tears started to roll down her cheeks as she wondered what was going to happen to her, what the men would do to her, why they had brought her to this house, what her Mother must have thought when she came to collect them and found only Amanda, and had Amanda found a security guard? Countless questions raced through her mind and she didn't have an answer for any of them.

Oscar now decided it was time for him to re-appear, which he did in a split second. He stood towering over Kate tied to the chair and she gasped as he appeared before her and immediately stopped crying. The last time she had seen him, he had been some distance away from her. Now he was right next to her and he was gigantic! As she stared at him, he slowly nestled down tucking his long legs underneath him and cuddled up to Kate, lowering his fluffy feathered head to rub against her cheek in the hope that it would help her to feel more secure. Although he could not talk to Kate, Oscar knew that he could get Kate to recognize that he was there to help her and that there would be an understanding between the two of them. Now, in this house, they would have the time to do just that.

Slowly Kate began to feel a little better. Tentatively she started to rub her cheek against Oscar's head and as she did so, she felt some of her confidence returning and didn't feel that her situation was quite so hopeless. Something told her that he was there for a good reason and that she could trust him because he was her friend. Where he had come from and how he could change big to small in the blink of an eye was something she wouldn't worry about at the moment. Instead, she talked away to him telling him what a marvellous bird he was, which is just what Oscar wanted to hear, and then she confessed that she didn't even know his name.

"I don't know your name," she said, "what shall I call you – what is your name?"

Oscar understood what she had said and immediately sent her a telepathic message containing his name. Kate was very surprised when, in her mind, she became instantly aware of the name Oscar and that it belonged to the bird by her side.

"Oscar, Oscar, that's it!" she cried. "Oh, Oscar – thank you for being here, I already feel so much better, but please say that you will stay, especially when those men come back – I just don't know what is going to happen to me."

Oscar knew that he would be with Kate at all times, but had no way of telling her, except with his huge amber eyes, so he continued to sit nestled up to her and to stare at her from time to time. The trust-building with her was important so he could give her confidence for what he knew would happen in the future.

It was not long before Fingers, The Cat and Freddie reappeared. When Kate and Oscar heard the front door opening, Oscar did his disappearing act and Kate felt him give her a gentle scratch again, to reassure her that he was there and that she need not feel afraid. Just then Freddie and The Cat came into the room where Kate was and they settled into two more comfortable chairs than the one they had given Kate.

"Now, little lady," said Freddie, in a voice which was anything but kind, "while you were eating your ice cream and staring at that silly bird in the zoo, exactly what did you hear while we were talking?"

Kate said nothing and knew that the scratch that came from Oscar meant that she should continue to say nothing. Freddie was not pleased and rose to his feet as he asked the question again and was greeted by a wall of silence from this girl.

"Come on, Freddie," said The Cat, "we've got some time and she will talk sooner or later." Kate, now feeling braver because of Oscar's presence, was determined that she was not going to talk, so she just sat in the chair with her eyes downcast.

In the meantime, Oscar, as well as giving the odd scratch to Kate to keep her courage up, was focusing very hard on communicating with Isia and Jenza. He had no idea where either of them were at that particular time, but knew that if he focused strongly enough he would get a message to them to be on guard telling them that he was going to need them and to be ready for more messages from him. At the rate things were moving he felt sure that, although he did not need them at the moment, he certainly was going to be counting on them for assistance in the not too distant future.

Far from the comfort of his Northern mountain home, Jenza was at that moment suffering from the heat in the middle of a desert keeping a watchful eye on a young Bedouin, Youssef, who was in danger of being kidnapped and killed by the outlawed tribe of Kahlil Abdullah, who lived by a code of terror, murder, captivity and on-going cruelty. Kahlil Abdullah could not tolerate these peace-loving Bedouins led by Youssef's father, Sheikh Adnan bin Ahmid. These people were a threat to Kahlil Abdullah's goals, which, simply put, were to see that the nomadic tribes inhabiting a particular desert region would come under his control. Once he had achieved this he would set his sights further afield!

Each tribal group was governed by a Sheikh and council of elders. Sheikh Adnan bin Ahmid, Youssef's father, was a respected and courageous leader with not only the support of his own tribal council, but also with the support of many other tribes and their councils. Kahlil Abdullah knew that he would cause an uprising if he attacked Sheikh Adnan bin Ahmid, an uprising he would find impossible to control. He had chosen the coward's way out and decided to kidnap Youssef and then demand a large ransom from Adnan bin Ahmid's tribe. This would be a huge set-back to Adnan bin Ahmid. Following receipt of the ransom from Adnan bin Ahmid's tribe, Kahlil Abdullah would then kill Youssef after the hand-over, while he was being reunited with his father.

Because of the impending situation and the disastrous results if it was allowed to continue, Jenza was there to ensure that the hated leader of the outlaw gang behind the planned kidnap and murder was stopped by any means before Youssef was harmed. He was protecting these peace-loving Bedouins and their leader, because they were spreading good will and good news throughout the desert and therefore Jenza endured the heat that was quite unnatural to him but longed for the cooler nights in the desert when the temperature dropped considerably. He tended to doze during the day and rest as much as possible to conserve his energy for nighttime when he knew the kidnappers would strike although unfortunately he did not know the exact date.

It was while he was dozing during the day that he was alerted to a sensory communication coming across thousands of miles. He knew right away that it was Oscar because all emissaries have a special code they use between all fellow emissaries. Because Oscar was his special friend, Jenza was more sensitive to the definite but distant code that was coming through and imprinting itself onto his brain. The tiger was alarmed – Oscar was in trouble! He knew this because the message he was receiving from Oscar was accompanied by definite negative vibes. Now Jenza was fully awake and his whiskers were twitching. Fortunately the message from Oscar was only a warning to stand by and await further communication. Jenza was thankful for this because he knew he must complete this important desert mission before he could leave. But he was troubled. He could not bear to think of his old friend or his friend's charge in danger but thankfully, Oscar's message was not yet critical.

This message now added to the worries Jenza had about Youssef. He had been watching the father and son in action from a safe distance and he realized how much the tribe and elders needed both the resolute, wise and courageous leader and the young man who appeared to be growing into a blueprint of his father. In many respects, Youssef seemed wise beyond his years and he had begun to demonstrate the resourcefulness and tenacity of his father.

Jenza knew that if anything happened to Adnan bin Ahmid it would set back the cause for freedom and choice from tyranny by at least 50 years, if not more. Jenza could see only too well what the future would be for all the tribes of the desert without a leader like Adnan bin Ahmid, and he did not like what he saw.

He must be alert and on guard and hope that his mission in the desert would be completed sooner rather than later, leaving him free to go and help his friend.

Isia was having a very lazy day doing nothing in particular. He had not been called on to act as an emissary for some time and he was enjoying his endless quest for food, which was quite plentiful around the coast of Vancouver Island in Western Canada. He had already caught two good size salmon that day and was way up at the top of a tree, feeling full and very contented. As was the case with Jenza and Oscar, Isia was a loner because he had to be. He was friendly towards other eagles, but they sensed there was something different about this bird, which made them wary about their contact with him. Isia would have liked more company but because he came from the Kingdom of Light he knew that his only real friends would be from there and not from the eagles on Earth. Still, it was sometimes a lonely existence because when eagles mate, they usually mate for life, and there is no room for such luxury in Isia's life as an emissary

As he watched the seagulls screaming at him and the other eagles to get away from their nesting areas, he remained on his perch and knew that they would not dare to chase him. The reasons the gulls were so distressed was, not because they feared for their own lives, but for the lives of their young. Screeching at and chasing the eagles was their only way of keeping their prying eyes out of their nests.

Suddenly, Isia became concerned. Oscar was trying to locate him! Instead of crouching on his perch at the top of the tree, he now stood upright, alarmed at the messages he was getting from his friend. Oscar was in trouble, but not dire trouble yet. This was a warning that told Isia and Jenza to be ready to receive a summons shortly. Free to go to Oscar's assistance at any time, Isia was now committed to keeping his sensory channels open and to be doubly alert.

At the end of an hour of hearing absolutely nothing out of Kate, in spite of a couple of slaps to her face, Freddie was now irate and ready to go further than just slapping her. The Cat knew this, but he also knew that they were in enough trouble as it was, especially concerning the dead man they had seen in the Blue Room at Ryerdale Hall. Whatever else he and Fingers were, they were not murderers. Neither one of them had blood on their hands and, as far as The Cat was concerned, they were not going to start now and he was very much afraid Kate's might be the first, as Freddie was getting very angry. Because he didn't know Freddie as well as he knew Fingers, The Cat was not sure how far Freddie's temper would take him.

"Right," said The Cat. "Freddie, this is getting us nowhere. Can we have a word in the kitchen?"

As they left, Kate, her heart pounding, was very thankful that she was not going to be on the receiving end of any more of Freddie's slaps at the moment.

As they reached the kitchen door, The Cat said, "I think we'll take our little guest out to the old hut in Pemberton Forest. It's not far from here and we can lock her up and leave her there until we've finished all our other business. She'll never get out of there and lack of food for a couple of days might just bring her to her senses."

Freddie was not happy with this plan, but he did understand the wisdom of what The Cat had said. "Little minx," he thought to himself, "I'll wait for another couple of days, and then she'll really know what's hit her by the time I get finished with her!"

The three men came through from the kitchen to tell Kate that they were going to take her to a place of safety where she would stay until they concluded their business and that if she behaved herself they might set her free. The Cat undid the ropes that bound Kate to the chair and she immediately rubbed her wrists and her hands flew into her pockets and she kept her eyes on the floor. As they left the house she tried to stay close to The Cat and fortunately sat with him again in the back of the car while Freddie drove and Fingers sat beside him. Once more the journey was completed in silence, with a periodic scratch from Oscar in Kate's pocket. She had no idea of where they were going and they seemed to take a long time getting there.

Freddie and The Cat had used this hut in Pemberton Forest on previous occasions to store stolen goods since it was well off the beaten track and could be kept padlocked. They left the road through the forest and finally arrived at the hut after a bumpy journey over a gravel and grass track. After Kate was dragged from the car she was pushed through the open door of the hut by Fingers and warned that there was nowhere for her to go until they came back. To be absolutely safe, they tied her to a chair again and left her, banging the door and padlocking it as they went.

Lord Ryerdale managed to get a noon flight home from his holiday resort, but Lady Ryerdale decided to stay on when he told her that once he had seen Burt's family, and had a look in the safe to satisfy Detective Superintendent Richardson's curiosity, he would be back to finish his holiday, probably within three or four days.

The Marchioness knew the story of The Mirendah and was also worried about her diamonds and emeralds, which were kept in the safe. She had seen the large diamond but since it was neither polished nor cut, it did not appeal to her and its enormous value meant little to her. Her husband was one of the richest men in the United Kingdom and she could have whatever she wanted in life without having to worry about the cost. Her only relief came with the thought that that the safe in their bedroom was so private and well hidden that she was sure nobody could possibly find it.

Lord Ryerdale arrived back in Manchester at three o'clock and Hayton, his chauffeur, was there to meet him. During the two-hour trip back to the Hall he quizzed Hayton about what had happened and was disappointed that the chauffeur could not tell him very much.

"No Sir," Hayton said, "they have found no evidence, either inside the Hall or in the gardens, of any robbery. Stuart and Dale are very upset because they blame themselves for Burt's death, but I don't see how they could have prevented what happened. Burt simply left the control room and went to the Keep without requesting any back-up. The other two had no idea what had happened until they discovered that the alarm had not been activated at eleven o'clock."

"Well, it is a sad day for all of us," said Lord Ryerdale. "What an awful thing to happen, and what his poor family must be going through. I must go over and see them first thing tomorrow Hayton, so perhaps you could have the car ready at nine o'clock."

"Very good, m'lord. Are you going to require the car again after we get back?"

"Probably not," replied Lord Ryerdale, "but you had better hang on, just in case, while I phone Detective Superintendent Richardson. We have to meet but I should think he will be coming out to The Hall."

"Right you are, Sir," replied Hayton as he pulled the car into the driveway of Ryerdale Hall. As they drove through the grounds and the Hall became visible, Andrew Ryerdale felt the same pleasant feeling of coming home that he always felt. He loved The Hall, probably because it had been in the family for so long. He had a smaller home in the Lake District, a rather palatial flat in London and a villa onGrand Bahama Island, but it was always wonderful to come home to The Hall.

His butler, Hawkins, was there to greet the master of the house as he bounded up the steps and after a quick word with his Estate Manager who was waiting just inside the door, Lord Ryerdale went straight to his study to put in a call to Detective Superintendent Richardson. As they had been told that he would be returning toThe Hall that day, several of the staff had come in to prepare his rooms for him and Madeleine, the cook, had put in an appearance to make him a cold salad lunch which he could eat picnic style while he was working.

Having arranged with the Detective Superintendent for him to come to The Hall so they could examine the safe together, Lord Ryerdale rang for Stuart and Dale to come to his office. He greeted them warmly when they arrived, full of sympathy for what had happened and what they had been through. He listened carefully to their story.

"Stuart, there is no good you and Dale blaming yourselves for what has happened. There was no way that you could have known that Burt would go to the Keep. He should have called one of you in to keep an eye on things while he went to see what was what, but he didn't and we may never know why. It had nothing to do with you," said Lord Ryerdale.

The three of them discussed the break-in and Burt's murder, but could still not come up with any conclusive answers. As they were about to go through the turn of events for the third time, Robert Haines, Lord Ryerdale's private secretary, rang to say that Detective Superintendent Richardson had arrived.

"Please show him in," said Lord Ryerdale and then turning to dismiss Stuart and Dale, he again told them that they were not to let this whole affair worry them and he stressed how pleased he was with the way they had managed everything in his absence.

"Nice to see you, Detective Superintendent," said Lord Ryerdale as he rose to greet him.

"Your Lordship . . ." murmured Detective Superintendent Richardson.

"Well, what do you want to do first?" asked Lord Ryerdale. "Shall we go upstairs and take a look at the safe?"

"What I would really like to do before going to the safe, is discuss the contents and perhaps you could explain to me why the safe had to remain such a secret," said Detective Superintendent Richardson.

"Well, there is a bit of a tale for the telling there," replied Lord Ryerdale, "and I will do my best to fill you in," he said, sitting down again and beckoning to Detective Superintendent Richardson to do the same.

"Have you ever heard of The Mirendah Diamond?" asked Lord Ryerdale.

"Vaguely," replied the Detective Superintendent. "As far as I can remember, about 150 years ago the diamond was stolen on its way to India, in a daring robbery. All the excitement gradually died down over the years and there's not much talk of it these days. The diamond has not been seen or heard of since." Detective Superintendent Richardson said all this in a matter-of-fact tone, showing no great interest in the fact that the subject had been brought up.

"Well," said Andrew, taking a rather large gulp of breath, which he hoped that Detective Superintendent would not notice. "The Mirendah Diamond is in that safe in our bedroom."

Lord Ryerdale continued, "The stone has been in my family for years and I have never been sure how we came by it in the first place. Of course it is priceless, although it is still not completely polished and cut. The reason you and the staff at The Hall here did not know about it was simply because I did not want word to get out at any time. I thought it best to continue to store it as my family has done in the past, without the outside world knowing.

Detective Superintendent Richardson was speechless. He could not understand how a man with an almost priceless possession could not tell the local police force who was charged with the safety of his home, that he had such a possession.

Lord Ryerdale guessed what the Detective Superintendent was thinking about and he smiled sheepishly. "Oh, I know, it was perhaps a foolish thing to do, but I expect we will find it quite safe and sound when we go and open the safe. Incidentally, the other items I had in that particular safe were some diamond and emerald jewelery passed down through the family and now belonging to my wife, and some old Bearer Bonds, which I suppose might be quite valuable now. Come on," he said, getting up, "lets go and have a look."

Detective Superintendent Richardson followed the owner from his office through the Great Banqueting Hall and into the passage that connected the Keep to the rest of the castle. His head was still spinning. The situation was incredible.

"You do realize, My Lord," Richardson remarked as they walked, "that even though you think no one knows about the diamond and where it is kept, that word will always get out about a thing of that value, especially in the criminal world.

What about the men who stole it originally? They must have known who they were working for. And the company that installed the safe for your father – somebody involved in that could have let fall a chance remark so that the whereabouts of the safe would be known."

Approaching the master bedroom along the Long Gallery, Lord Ryerdale was feeling very foolish and regretted that he had never done anything about making the diamond more secure. He knew what the Detective Superintendent said made sense. He should have told the police and his insurance company about it long ago and not listened to his father's arguments about protecting the good name of the family.

As they opened the heavy oak door and went into the bedroom, Andrew Ryerdale headed over to the large wardrobe on the opposite side of the room and signalled to Detective Superintendent Richardson that he needed some help. The two of them managed to move the wardrobe along the wall. Finally the safe was revealed and the Detective Superintendent had to admit to himself that it could only have been found by someone who knew exactly where it was.

"Any minute now," said Lord Ryerdale, as he dialed in the combination that would unlock the safe, "and we will see that this has been a lot of fuss about nothing."

The door of the safe opened to reveal that it was completely empty.

Chapter Five

Twists and Turns

During his flight from the Hall on the night of the robbery, Max was frantically trying to work out the best way of handling the mess he had got himself into. Not only had he failed miserably to catch up with Fingers and The Cat, he had murdered a man. He knew it had been by accident, but would the police have seen it that way if he had been unable to make his getaway? The rope he had used for his escape was still there as proof that somebody had broken into the Keep. Due to his unfortunate bungling, he had no proof as to whether Fingers and The Cat had carried out their part of the plan but, knowing them as he did, he thought it very likely that they were by now miles away congratulating themselves and discussing how to get the most money out of their ill-gotten gains. To add insult to injury, his hasty slide down the rope had scraped all the skin from the palms of his hands and they were still bleeding. But the biggest problem of all was what he was going to tell Roger Corr?

During the two hours it took him to drive to the Corr hideout, an old disused warehouse on the outskirts of Manchester, Max struggled to come up with a story for Roger that would at least guarantee that he would walk out of the warehouse alive. He knew, from his fifteen years with the gang, that Roger had a wicked temper and was not beyond killing someone in a fit of rage. Not only would Roger have to accept the loss of the two best burglars in his gang, but also the fact that the diamond he had been planning for months to steal had been lost because of Max's stupidity. How forgiving would he be? All these thoughts swam around in Max's head as he drove towards Manchester. He had to admit to himself that he was getting old. If he wasn't, he would have been much more capable and fit than he had been this evening. As far as he could see, he had only two choices. The first would be to go into hiding and spend his entire life on the run hoping that Roger would not find him, with the knowledge that Roger would never stop looking. No, that was not an option. The Corr Gang was his 'family' and he knew no other way of life and he was too old to start thinking about a new one. The second choice would be to go to the warehouse and face up to Roger and take the consequences.

Roger was a harsh leader with a foul temper, who expected absolute loyalty from his people. He gave orders without thinking about the dangers that might be involved for the members of his gang, and he expected those orders to be obeyed. On the other hand, he himself was quite prepared to go on missions with the gang and face exactly the same dangers he expected them to face. His only redeeming feature was that he was generous to a fault and had a grudging admiration for his gang members. He had never yet harmed any one of them. Was that all about to change when he heard what Max had to tell him?

There were, in all, six other members of the gang apart from Roger, his son Big Al and Max himself. These members were Fingers, The Cat, Fatty, The Snake, Joey Lang and Johnny Graize and Max knew them all pretty well. Like him, they had all been with Roger for a long time and were like a big family rather than a gang of criminals. The others had also made mistakes, some as serious as Max's problem tonight, and they were still alive to tell the tale. All these thoughts led Max to the conclusion that the only thing he could do now was to face

Roger and tell him what had happened. Hopefully he might stand a chance of emerging from the mess in one piece.

Max finally reached the warehouse, his still bleeding hands barely able to hold the wheel of the car and he went straight to look for Roger. He found him in the office together with Big Al. This made Max feel slightly more hopeful, as Big Al very often had a calming effect on his father. After a cursory greeting, Max sat on a nearby chair with his hands upturned and related his story to Roger exactly as it happened, hiding nothing. As he finished his dismal account of the night's events he sat waiting for Roger to explode, but Roger started pacing the floor looking very serious, and giving nothing away. Big Al sat back in his chair, nervously sipping at a drink as the tension heightened. The room was quiet and still except for the ticking of the wall clock, which seemed louder than usual. Max could hardly bear it. His fists clenched down beside his body, now stiff with stress and tension, his eyes darted between Roger and Big Al, desperately trying to read their thoughts.

Finally, and almost in a whisper, Roger said, "I am disappointed in you Max - very disappointed. You should have made damn sure before you went in there that you knew which room you should be heading for. You had your mobile, why didn't you phone on your way there? Luckily, I had the idea that all would not go well with you and I alerted Fatty and The Snake who were in that general area. After some clever investigation, they learned from a chap called Freddie Bendell that a robbery had been committed at Ryerdale Hall and that the thieves had absconded with a heist worth millions of pounds.

"Thanks to some excellent work by Fatty and The Snake, I know that Fingers and The Cat did the job and I know where they are now." He gritted his teeth and added, almost as an afterthought, "and those two traitors really don't know what they have coming to them."

Roger then came towards Max and said, in a menacing voice, "And I don't suppose you know either, my dear Max, what might be coming to you. I'm not going to do anything with you at the moment, but if the police catch up with you, as I am sure they might, then you will be on your own and you won't get a scrap of help from me." With that triumphant note in his voice, Roger turned on his heels and strode out of the office.

"You've been lucky, Max," sighed Al as his body slumped with release of the tension, "he must have a soft spot for you! If I were you I would get lost before he comes back and changes his mind."

Max mumbled some kind of agreement to Al's remarks and quickly made himself scarce. What he needed now was to have a drink, a very stiff drink, see to his hands, and go to bed for some much needed sleep. After that there would be time to worry about Roger, the police and what was going to happen to him.

Having convinced herself that somebody would have to go and get help and that she wasn't nearly brave enough to stay behind instead of Kate, Amanda went off in search of a security guard. Because of what they had heard the three men talking about, she was anxious not to leave Kate by herself for any longer than she had to. So she ran in the direction of the main offices of the zoo, frantically looking around all the while to see if she could find the help she needed before she got there. Remembering all the guards they had seen on their way round the zoo earlier, it was frustrating that there was not a single one to be seen now.

It was a good four minutes before she spotted the familiar uniform of a security guard member outside the elephant compound and she rushed up to him. Amanda launched into her story so quickly that the words almost fell over one another in her effort to get them out. The guard held up his hands and told her to speak more slowly but, as she told him again what had happened, she realized how far-fetched it all sounded.

The security guard looked at her and didn't know what to think. Here was this frightened girl talking to him about three men, a jewel robbery, a dead body and the friend she had left sitting on the bench outside the ostrich enclosure. His first thought was that there was no way that this could happen in a perfectly normal place like a zoo, but the more Amanda repeated her story, the more he felt there must be something in it. He agreed to go with her and see Kate and make sure she was safe.

He started to walk towards the ostrich enclosure, with Amanda pleading with him to go faster, but there was no sign of Kate or the three men when they got there, and Amanda began to feel really scared. She hoped against hope that Kate had just moved on to look at the next lot of animals, but there was no sign of her. The security guard was beginning to see himself being dragged from one part of the zoo to another, looking for a girl who might not even exist. He decided that it was probably some kind of hoax.

As he steered Amanda back to the ostriches he told her that he was not going any further. In spite of her pleadings, he still suspected the whole thing was all in her imagination. Even if any of it was true, it would be a matter for the police and he decided that he would report it to the duty manager before he went home, in about ten minutes time. He told Amanda this and left her there feeling absolutely helpless and frantic with worry about what might have happened to Kate. As she was having a final look around to make sure there was no sign of her friend, she suddenly noticed that the smaller ostrich they had been looking at and admiring seemed to have gone. She went a bit further along the fence and looked for the golden coloured ostrich among the other birds, but there was no sign of it. Amanda thought to herself that if she'd told the guard that one of the zoo's ostriches was missing he would have torn the zoo apart looking for it. Surely, what might have happened to Kate was more important than that!

She suddenly caught sight of her watch and realized it was nearly the time the two girls were supposed to meet Kate's mother outside the zoo. The thought of being with a grown-up who would believe her story and take some of the responsibility away from her made Amanda feel better and she ran towards the zoo exit, where she almost collided with Mrs. Foster.

"Aunt Marianne," Amanda cried as the tears she had been trying to hold back started to roll down her cheeks, "Kate's disappeared!"

"Disappeared, what do you mean Amanda, disappeared?" asked Kate's mother with a feeling of dread washing over her. "Are you sure she hasn't just gone to see some other animals and will turn up in a minute?" Even as she said it, Marianne knew that it was much more serious than that, judging by the state Amanda was in. Amanda told her what had happened and Marianne realized that it was not a story Amanda could have invented. She felt cold and clammy with fear about what could have happened to her daughter. In spite of this, her motherly instincts prevailed and she realized that Amanda had been through enough, so Marianne fought down her own fears as much as she could to comfort Amanda. They went back into the zoo and made their way to the ostrich enclosure and the bench where Kate had been sitting when Amanda left her. Amanda showed Marianne where the three men had been sitting, and also explained about the missing ostrich.

"Amanda," said Marianne, "I want you to go over to the bench where the three men were sitting and start talking to yourself in a normal voice. There are not many people about at the moment, so no one will hear you." Reluctantly, Amanda did as she was asked while Marianne sat on the bench Kate and Amanda had used. Amanda started to talk and Marianne could hear quite well what she was saying. The more she listened, the more the horror of it all sank in. Kate, her daughter, must have been kidnapped!

Now that Amanda's story made sense, Marianne knew they had to go to the police. Beside herself with worry as to what had happened to Kate and absolutely furious that the security guard had refused to take Amanda's story seriously, Mrs. Foster set off with Amanda to the main offices. Here she would get them to call the police as quickly as they could and also make an official complaint against the guard, who had probably made the situation worse by refusing to believe Amanda.

Refusing the chairs that were offered after they had been shown into the office of the duty manager, Marianne quickly gave an outline of Kate's disappearance and possible kidnap. The duty manager called the local police straight away. While they were waiting for them to arrive, Marianne got Amanda to repeat what she had told the security guard and how he had reacted. Amanda did this and then added at the end, with just a touch of spite in her voice, "and you will be pleased to know that your precious golden ostrich is missing too!"

The duty manager, who had been listening intently to all that Amanda had to say, looked aghast at Amanda's last remark.

"Golden ostrich?" he said, "but Amanda, we don't have such a bird at the zoo."

"Oh, yes you do," contradicted Amanda. "Kate and I were admiring it for a while because we thought he was so different and quite gorgeous," replied Amanda. "He seemed to be watching us too. When I returned and couldn't find Kate, and was having a good look round I noticed that the golden ostrich had gone and that only the ordinary ostriches were there."

Now the duty manager was quite alarmed at Amanda's convictions. This girl was already in a distressed and agitated state and he didn't want to cause further stress by insisting that the zoo just had ordinary ostriches. He simply had no idea where Amanda had got the notion about a golden ostrich - as far as he knew, no such bird existed in the world, never mind Chester Zoo!

"O.K.," agreed the duty manager. "We will look into the matter of the ostrich disappearance. He picked up the phone and issued instructions for someone to go and count the number of ostriches in the ostrich enclosure. There was no reference made to a specific bird so as not to alarm Amanda. He replaced the receiver, hoping that he had said enough to calm Amanda's over-active imagination. Even if it didn't, she didn't question him further and taking a second or so to compose himself, he turned to Marianne.

"Now, Mrs. Foster, I am very concerned about your daughter and I am sure the police will be here in a few minutes. They will more than likely want you and Amanda down at the station to give them a statement. One of our staff will drive you there, wait for you while you make your statements, and bring you back to your car afterwards. Obviously, I will follow the case closely."

The police arrived almost immediately after the duty manager had finished speaking. Before going off to investigate the sight where Kate disappeared, one of the constables mentioned that Detective Superintendent Richardson was expecting Marianne and Amanda at the police station. The duty manager went with them to the zoo staff car he had put at their disposal and said to Marianne, "I can assure you, Mrs. Foster, that the offending security guard will be severely disciplined for his conduct. He should have stayed with Amanda, even if he felt that her story was a bit far-fetched, and then contacted me immediately. Please accept my apologies."

Amanda managed a wan smile as she followed Kate's mother out to the car. She was feeling very tired as well as being beside herself with worry about her friend. "How could I have left Kate?" she mumbled to herself, and felt tears pricking at the back of her eyelids.

Detective Inspector Jim Jones was reading some notes he had made the previous night at Ryerdale Hall. He had slept little, but that didn't matter to Jim. Detective Inspector Jones was in his mid thirties and like D.I. Bradford, he was assigned to the team led by Detective Superintendent Richardson.

Jim really enjoyed his work and was always looking for extra evidence, even if it meant extra work. Still a bachelor, he didn't have family responsibilities to consider so it didn't matter to him how much time he spent away from his home. Eager to learn and climb the ladder of police success, he could not have had a better mentor than John Richardson, who was happy to encourage Jim, but he was a stern taskmaster and would not tolerate any sloppiness from his subordinates. Both Jim and Don Bradford knew this and it was quite a challenge keeping up with the high standards expected.

Detective Superintendent Richardson had just returned to the police station when the call from the duty manager at the zoo came in and was answered by D.I. Jones. After hearing from Detective Inspector Jones about the disappearance of Kate and an outline of the conversation the girls had overheard, in particular reference to the name of 'Fingers', he was more than interested in meeting Marianne and Amanda and learning the full story. He was hoping that this could be the fresh evidence he needed to find out who had committed the murder and theft at Ryerdale Hall and what had happened to The Mirendah Diamond and the rest of the items taken from the safe.

He felt that the whole incredible story was too unreal not to be taken seriously. He could not imagine how anybody could have made up a story about the disappearance of a friend from the middle of a busy zoo in broad daylight, to say nothing of an ostrich, though he was inclined to take that bit of the tale with a pinch of salt. Having two daughters himself, he knew that sometimes imagination tended to take over from reality. But the mention of a body and a diamond had to be more than a coincidence.

Not knowing quite what to expect, he had one of his staff make a pot of tea, which had just been brewed when Marianne and Amanda walked through the door. The look of shock on the faces of both of them told him that hot tea was just what was needed. Once settled in his comfortable office, Amanda went through the whole story again with several interruptions from Marianne, but Detective Superintendent Richardson was a patient man. He was particularly interested in hearing more about the three men who had been sitting near the girls.

"Amanda," he said, "I want you to think very carefully and tell me again exactly what you heard while you were sitting there with Kate."

"There was one man called Fingers, because one of the other men told him to shut up and called him by that name. He was saying something about a man lying on a sofa, twisted and that he didn't like looking at dead bodies. Then the man, who told Fingers to shut up, said something about 'sparklers' and eight million. The third man interrupted and called the man talking about the 'sparklers', Freddie. This man, Freddie, said something about...it sounded like 'Miranda'. Then the third man was talking about Miranda being polished, and then he started to talk about Bearer Bonds."

"Very interesting," said Detective Superintendent Richardson. When he had first heard the name Fingers mentioned, he knew right away that this had been the work of the Corr Gang and that Fingers and The Cat were definitely responsible for the robbery and possibly the murder. What Amanda had told him confirmed those thoughts. He was quite careful to avoid any kind of comment about the Corr Gang and the robbery, or the murder, because he knew just how anxious Marianne was about Kate. He knew that in all their previous robberies, the gang had never been known to murder anyone, but he also knew that Roger Corr had a terrible temper which could have led to murder if he had been directly involved in the job, and that really bothered him. Now, apparently an innocent girl was in the hands of these men and he was more than a little concerned as to what would happen to her. But now at least they had some hard evidence to work on.

After more questions for both Marianne and Amanda, statements from both of them were taken down. Detective Superintendent Richardson assured Marianne that these statements would be given to his team of detectives to work on right away and he would keep in touch with the family. He thought it best to comfort them by saying that if Kate had been kidnapped, these men were not the kind to seriously harm her. Unfortunately, that did nothing to make Marianne feel any better and it was all she could do to keep from crying and breaking down. While she was at the police station she had phoned her husband, who had agreed to drive out to the zoo and take them home, so, after the statements had been signed, she was anxious to get back to the zoo.

Remembering to thank the Superintendent for his help in advance, she said she hoped she would be hearing from him soon with news of Kate. Marianne led the way to the car comforting Amanda, who was also struggling because she knew how Kate's mother must be feeling. What was worse was that she also battled with guilt feelings because leaving Kate in the first place had caused all this to happen. They sat in silence on the way back to the zoo, each with their own worrying thoughts, to find Mark was there waiting for them with Brian, Amanda's father. Brian had driven Mark there, as Marianne's car was already at the zoo. Marianne was so relieved she just collapsed against her husband, who held her tightly. Amanda was overjoyed to see her father and ran to him with outstretched arms. No one spoke much afterwards, except to bid each other goodbye and get into their own cars. Mark promised Brian that they would be in touch the minute they heard anything from the police.

It was nearly five o'clock in the afternoon when Detective Superintendent Richardson had finally seen Marianne and Amanda out of the station door.   He went back inside to try and piece a few things together, even though he was feeling exhausted. It was now clear that the Corr Gang was responsible for the robbery, although he still couldn't see the two cat burglars being involved in murder. The immediate problem was that Fingers and The Cat had a young girl with them and he had no idea where they could be. He had to find more evidence. A touch of the intercom on his desk summoned Detective Inspector Jim Jones.

"Jim, I want you to arrange for a bulletin to go out asking anyone who was at the zoo today and near the ostrich enclosure between twelve and one o'clock to contact us immediately, and then arrange to interview everyone who comes forward.

Amanda did say there had not been many people around them at the time, but you never know. Also, I need someone to go back to the Hall at around seven o'clock because Lord Ryerdale will have an envelope that I need as soon as possible. And another thing, you might like to get someone to look up the files we have on the Corr Gang in the data bank – each individual member. Apparently Fingers, and presumably The Cat, were in on this robbery, but those two have never been murderers. See what you can dig up as quickly as you can."

"Right away Sir," replied Jim Jones. He too was worn out, but with a young girl missing and the possibility that something he might find would help to trace her, he felt revived and ready to give everything his best shot.

When he had the office to himself again, Detective Superintendent Richardson pushed back his chair and put his feet up on the desk. He ran over in his mind everything that had happened since his call-out to Ryerdale Hall the previous night. Although the empty safe had proved that the motive for the break-in was robbery, Lord Ryerdale had asked him to keep quiet about The Mirendah because he would rather the newspapers didn't get word of it. Eventually, Richardson had agreed to this, but he told Lord Ryerdale that he wanted an itemized list of everything that was in the safe, together with descriptions of the emerald, diamond and ruby jewellery and The Mirendah. He would then copy the list for circulation to other forces after removing any mention of The Mirendah.

All this, of course, did not bring him any nearer to finding out who had murdered Burt. The autopsy report had been sent over, as promised by Dr. Lloyd, but it did not show anything that would help them further in any way. It just confirmed that

Burt had been shot, that the approximate time of death was half past ten, and that after the murder the body had been moved from the Long Gallery to the sofa in the Blue Room. There had been no fingerprints on the grappling hook but they had found traces of skin on the rope and this meant they were looking for a man with very sore hands! He was disappointed that nothing had turned up in the garden. Unfortunately the soil was too dry for any footprints to have been left, and there was no evidence as to where the getaway car had been parked. At the moment, his only hope lay in being able to find Kate with Fingers and The Cat and he turned to check Amanda's statement again. He knew that time would be limited because he guessed that they would be trying to leave the country. He had no idea yet that the two cat burglars had split from the Corr Gang, and that there was all the more reason to hurry because it was turning out to be a race between the police and Roger Corr to get to the renegades first. Had Richardson known this he would have been even more worried about what was happening to Kate.

— The Diamond Talisman —

— Chapter Six —

Counter Strikes

After the noise of the car had disappeared, the silence was deafening. Kate looked around her and thought of Freddie's last remark about behaving herself. What else could she possibly do in a place like this? Still not feeling very brave, even though she knew Oscar was in her pocket Kate became anxious, not only because she was bound and helpless but also because of the way the men had treated her. If they treated her this badly while not knowing how much of their conversation in the zoo she had overheard, what would they do to her if they found out how much she had heard?

Suddenly Oscar was standing before her, stretching himself after his somewhat cramped journey. Kate felt a huge sense of relief sweep over her. "Oh Oscar," she cried, "How are we going to get out of this mess? I am so frightened of what those men might do when they come back." In reply, Oscar set about pecking as hard as he could at the ropes that bound her. "Isia," thought Oscar to himself, as he worked to free Kate's hands from the tight rope, "I need you now, my friend. I need you to trace us from the zoo to the house where we were first held captive and then to wherever this hut is situated, but hurry – please hurry." Kate had no idea that all this was going on inside Oscar's head, but she began to feel the rope slacken and she started to twist her wrists. With one more tug from Oscar's strong beak her hands were free and she was able to untie the ropes around her feet. With Oscar's help, she made short work of the rather shoddy knots Fingers had put in the rope.

Kate now realized that if Oscar could disappear when he was in the ostrich enclosure at the zoo and re-appear in the pocket of her shirt as a small bundle of fluff, he could undoubtedly get himself out of the hut. But what Oscar could do with his special powers, she could not, so she had to find a means of escape. By what little daylight was left, she started to search for a way out of the hut. There was only one door, which was securely padlocked and there were three very small panes of glass which let in a little light, but they were not proper windows so there was no way out there. Opposite the door she came to what she guessed was some sort of kitchen. There was a small camp stove and several dirty pots and pans. As she crossed the floor from there to check the last small pane of glass at the side of the hut she felt the floor give way slightly beneath her right foot. Further investigation by both Kate and Oscar showed a rotten piece of floorboard. Excitedly, Kate pulled at the end of the board and it started to come up, revealing plain good old earth underneath. She decided that this could be the way out if she could pull another couple of boards up and then dig out the soft earth below, she could perhaps make a hole big enough for her to get under the wall.

Oscar did not need to be told what she was thinking and before she could stoop down again to start pulling at the boards, he placed his sinewy leg and large two-toed foot on the board. He hooked the vicious looking claw-like nail under the floorboard and with one pull, he ripped the board up. Kate could only stand in amazement and watch Oscar at work. She had never had any particular interest in ostriches before and knew very little about them. When she saw Oscar's display of strength and how quickly he worked, she felt a great respect for this bird, which could be so gentle one minute and so strong the next.

It was not long before Oscar had not only the floorboards up, but also a neat pile of earth on top of the discarded boards and a hole leading under the wall of the hut that was large enough for Kate to get through. He stepped back to admire his handiwork and was rewarded with a hug from Kate. Without a second thought, Kate went down on her hands and knees and began to wriggle her way through the hole and out of the hut. Oscar had done a great job and it did not take her too long to get through, even though the small tunnel was a bit tight. Once outside, she took a grateful gulp of fresh air and looked around. The hut was situated in a small clearing, surrounded by trees that seemed very tall and menacing to Kate. The ground under the trees was a solid mass of brambles. What worried her was that there was no sign of any path to or from the hut through the trees and yet they had arrived by car and she did not recall having to walk very far to the hut. What she did not know was that a section of the brambles was false, and could be moved when those in the know wanted access to the hut. While she was thinking about this, she heard a swoosh of feathers and Oscar appeared, towering above her.

"Well, Oscar, what are we going to do now? I know we're out of the hut, but I can't see any way through these trees, so I suppose we shall have to start pushing our way through the brambles," she said, disappointed at finding yet another problem to overcome. Oscar, of course, knew that they were not going anywhere until Isia appeared, and he was wondering how long he would have to wait for his friend. In the meantime, he had to try and persuade Kate to remain where they were, which he was sure would not be for too long. It was so difficult, not being able to speak to her. Instead, he lifted his beautiful wing and cast it protectively around Kate's shoulders, gently hugging her to him, preventing her from starting out on her own.

Kate sensed that Oscar did not want her to leave for the moment, although she was at a loss to understand why. To her it seemed that time was very important and all she wanted to do was to get out of this horrible place and go home before those three men came back. Her mind was in a turmoil thinking again about what might have happened to Amanda, or wondering if her parents knew she was missing. More importantly, she really wanted to report the pieces of conversation she and Amanda had heard in the zoo so that the men could be stopped, especially if they had been involved in a murder. She was about to pull herself away from the comfort of Oscar's wing, when out of nowhere Isia appeared, muttering to himself in his high-pitched squeaky voice, which seemed quite ridiculous for such a large bird.

Isia perched himself at the end of a large branch not far from their left side and stretched his wings to their full span of nearly eight feet. Kate had never seen a bird with such enormous wings. Oscar took a couple of steps towards Isia and put his long neck out to greet his old friend. Kate looked on, bewildered. She had no idea what the bird was and what it was doing here. While Isia was squeaking away, Oscar was emitting some very strange, mournful sounds. Kate had to assume that this was their way of talking to each other. She suddenly had the same feeling that she used to get on her walks with Lulu, her dog, sitting and looking at the clouds in the sky. Looking back, it appeared that the emotions she felt then had been some sort of sign or omen of what was to come. Never in her wildest dreams, would she have imagined herself in the middle of a forest with a golden ostrich and this other odd-looking bird, neither of which were normally to be found in the United Kingdom. Unlike Oscar, Isia looked very fierce with his great white head, piercing eyes and hooked beak and she was just a little bit afraid of him. Oscar immediately sensed this and spoke again to Isia in his own peculiar way. Isia flew down from his branch and waddled in a very ungainly way to Kate's feet. Tentatively, she reached out her hand to his head, expecting any minute to be attacked by that fearful beak, but Isia behaved like a lamb and found he rather liked Kate fondling his feathered head. Still a bit nervous, Kate lowered herself down so that she was level with Isia's head and she made herself look into his fierce eyes, which were now radiating a warm glow and she felt herself relaxing.

Oscar too, had come closer to her and using the same telepathy he had used when he wanted Kate to know his name, he told her about Isia. At that moment, Kate knew Isia's name and that he was a bald eagle from Canada. She was starting to get used to this business of thoughts being put into her mind, but she still wished she could talk to these two strange birds properly and find out why Isia was there. She now realized that Oscar had been trying to keep her there because they had to wait for Isia, but why that should be so, Kate had no idea. She had also accepted that for whatever reason, Oscar was there to help her and she knew she could trust him. Because of Oscar she accepted Isia and, in spite of her fear, made friends with him. Beyond that, she was not sure what was going to happen next. One thing was certain, they had to move and get away before Freddie, Fingers and The Cat came back.

Reading her thoughts, Oscar unexpectedly dropped to the ground so that his back was level with Kate. He bent his head around towards her and then towards his back. While she was trying to work out what he meant, Isia landed on Oscar's back as if he was preparing to go for a ride. He then hopped off Oscar's back and flapped his way back on again and settled his gaze on Kate. In the meantime, Oscar kept turning round swinging his neck back and pointing his beak towards his back and Isia. Finally, Kate got the message. She was supposed to get up on Oscar's back! Gingerly she took a step towards the great bird and Isia hopped off again, looking as though he was preparing for flight. Kate climbed awkwardly onto Oscar's back, not quite knowing how she was supposed to sit and what she was going to hold onto. After a few minutes of trying different ways, she finally settled for legs astride, as if riding a horse, quite near to Oscar's neck so that she could put her arms around it. She found his feathers soft and comfortable and felt very high up when he had risen and was standing again.

The strange party was ready to go. Isia took off and flew just above the tops of the trees. Oscar started to run and went straight towards the trees and brambles that faced the main entrance of the hut and plunged into them. Before Kate could even think about how the brambles must be scratching his legs, they were out again on the other side onto a rough track, which was obviously where Freddie had driven the car. Not far in front of him was Isia pacing his flight with Oscar's speed, which was much faster now that the brambles had been left behind.

As Oscar gathered speed Kate's grasp tightened around his neck. She was surprised at how smooth the ride was, and also that she was warm in spite of the cold night breeze. Not only did Oscar's feathers protect her from the cold, he was going so fast that a sort of jet stream developed that passed over the top of both him and Kate. His strong legs made such giant strides; he was able to run at nearly forty miles per hour. Had there been someone watching them, they would have thought that Oscar and Kate looked like some kind of weird aircraft about to take off! Isia was the only one who knew where they were going so he had to stay not too far in front of Oscar, so that Oscar would not lose sight of him.

After Isia had wished himself from his perch in Canada to the zoo in the United Kingdom, as Oscar had told him, he went straight to the ostrich enclosure. There he was able to find Oscar's aura, which was still in the air, even though Oscar had gone. Since he had known him for so long, it was not difficult for Isia to pick up Oscar's aura and as soon as he had it, he followed the trail that led directly to the fence where Oscar had disappeared into Kate's shirt pocket. He then had to keep fairly close to the ground to follow the aura, which had grown faint with the change in Oscar's size, but it was still definitely there. This meant that Isia had to fly quite low as he followed the trail out of the zoo and into the car park where Kate had been forced into the car.

Although it was late in the day, there were still a fair number of people around and they stared in disbelief when they saw this strange bird flying so low. Some ran for cover, thinking that Isia might be dangerous but others just stood and watched. A few people went in search of somebody from the zoo, thinking that this bird must have escaped. One man even telephoned a friend of his, who was a keen birdwatcher, to ask him whether he knew what the bird was. This friend was very excited at the thought of seeing an unknown species of bird and hurried, with a few of his fellow birdwatchers, towards the area of the sighting. Inevitably, one of them contacted the local paper, and by the time Isia had followed the trail of the car and Oscar to the house where Fingers and the Cat had been staying and where they had kept Kate as a prisoner, there was quite a crowd heading that way too.

Isia had just discovered, by flying round the house and looking in through all the windows, that it was empty when he became aware of the interest he had caused and decided it was time to do a disappearing act. Like Oscar, he could make himself smaller and so could not be seen from his hiding place behind the chimney up on the roof. This left a lot of puzzled people with cameras and binoculars standing in the road with nothing to look at!

Keeping a wary eye out, Isia, still unseen on his perch on the roof of the house, began to feel quite irritable. The clock was ticking and Oscar was waiting for him to get there as soon as possible but he really could not do much while those silly people with cameras were in front of the house. Finally, after half an hour of trying to find this strange bird, people reluctantly packed up their cameras and binoculars and left. Once they had gone, Isia went back to his usual size and flew around the lower windows of the house just to confirm again that Oscar had been there. Picking up his aura on the path outside the front door, he started to follow it again. The trail took him out of the village and over green fields and rolling hills with trees and farms dotted all over the landscape. How different from his native Canada where, in most places, there were endless stretches of millions of trees as far as the eye could see, all growing close together.

Fortunately, it had turned into a calm, clear night with just a hint of moonlight, making his journey pleasant and easy. It wasn't too long before he came to Pemberton Forest, where the hut was situated. Following Oscar's aura, he circled the forest until he came to the rough road that had provided access for Freddie, Fingers and The Cat with their prisoner. Keeping low, he followed the track but was suddenly confronted by a wall of trees. He was unable to fly through so it was a matter of soaring over the top. The wall of trees was only about six feet deep and Isia knew they would not present a problem for Oscar when the time came for them to leave the clearing and move on.

Any reunion with his old friend was always good, and it was especially so on this occasion, as they had not seen each other for quite a while. Although he did not mix with them very often, Isia was used to humans and knew that he presented a rather fearsome sight when first meeting one of these funny two-legged creatures, so he had to do his best to look a little less daunting for this young girl who had become Oscar's charge.

By the time the flying and running party of two birds and one girl reached the outskirts of Chilfray, dawn was just beginning to break and as there was nobody about at that time of day, it made life a lot easier for Oscar and Isia. After all, Oscar couldn't have done his shrinking trick with Kate on his back! Isia led them straight to the house, where Oscar dropped down to let Kate dismount. Isia went back to his hiding place behind the chimney on the roof, to be ready if he was needed later. He certainly didn't want to stay as his normal size and risk attracting the same sort of crowd as he had the last time he was flying around Chilfray. As she climbed down from Oscar's back, Kate felt a bit stiff, but she was calm now that she knew she could rely on Oscar and Isia no matter what happened.

Although the house looked empty, Kate supposed that the men could be asleep. She discounted this, however, when she discovered there was no car in the driveway and went up to the front door and turned the handle and, of course, it was locked. She looked at the nearest window and noticed that the catch was off the hook on one of the windows. Turning to Oscar, she asked if he could disappear and re-appear inside the house and push the window open so that she could get in. Oscar needed no second bidding, and in a few minutes Kate had climbed through the window and was standing in a sparsely furnished room. To confirm that no one was about she checked the house to make sure, with Oscar following. Indeed, there was nobody there. Would they be back, she wondered, or should she be trying to find a police station? If she did go to the police, would the few phrases about a diamond and a body be enough for them to find and arrest her three captors? Now that she had Oscar and Isia to help her, it might be much better to try and find out more about the men and where they had hidden the spoils. She would be able to lead the police straight to them, so that the jewels and bonds could eventually be returned to their rightful owner.

No, she had to try and find the stolen goods. She knew that they must be in the house somewhere because the three men were discussing the sum of money they could get for the gems. If that was the case, she thought, they would want to have the jewellery available if an offer was made and the buyers needed to see the real thing before the deal was finalized. She decided that she had to risk a more thorough inspection and hoped that it could be completed before Fingers, The Cat and Freddie returned.

Carefully, she searched each room, delving through cupboards, drawers, behind doors, into corners and under beds – anywhere that might prove a hiding place for something. Finally, after a thorough search she had turned up nothing and she found herself in the kitchen that was her last hope.

Oscar, who had been watching all this, went over to the fridge and tapped his beak on it, signaling for her to open the door, which she did without delay. Nothing – completely empty. "Did these people ever eat?" she wondered to herself as she stared at the empty fridge. Oscar's actions had spurred her on but the disappointment of finding the fridge empty made her feel pessimistic again. Her next target was the microwave oven – nothing. Finally, with a heavy heart and no expectations, she went to the wall oven. It was not empty. A large meat pan occupied the middle shelf and when Kate pulled it, instead of meat there was a leather briefcase. Excitedly, she pulled the briefcase out of the pan and tried to undo it, until she realized that it was locked and she didn't have a key! In a tantrum she flung the briefcase onto the floor in front of Oscar.

"Oscar, we finally find something and it can't be opened," she cried, unable to hide her disappointment. Oscar simply picked up the bag with his beak and placed it back in the meat pan, nudging Kate to put the pan back in the oven. As she was doing this, she felt the briefcase again. It didn't feel as though there was anything hard in there, like jewellery, but there was definitely a bundle of something, she guessed. After she had shut the oven, Kate looked at Oscar again, hands on her hips, just as though he was spoiling all her fun! In reply Oscar turned round and led the way out of the kitchen, through the backdoor and into the garden. He, of course, knew exactly what Kate was thinking and he decided it would be much better if they surprised the three men, rather than remain in the house waiting for them to come back. The small summerhouse at the end of the garden was the obvious answer. Putting his wing around Kate and nudging her in that direction, the two of them walked towards the gazebo.

The summerhouse was very basic and there was no door, but there was enough cover for Kate to remain hidden and Oscar could always make himself smaller or disappear if he had to. They could see the drive at the front of the house from their hiding place so they would know exactly when the men came back. Kate and Oscar made themselves as comfortable as possible and started to wait, hoping that it was not going to be for too long. Kate found herself wondering if the three men would come back at all. But as Freddie had promised to return to the hut in the forest to release her when they had completed their business, she supposed they would still be using this house as a base.

On the previous evening, Detective Inspector Jones had written and posted his two bulletins as soon as he had received Detective Superintendent Richardson's instructions. So by six o'clock, the APBs (All Points Bulletins) had been sent to all police stations across the country including those at ports, airports and the Channel Tunnel and this meant that Fingers and The Cat would not be able to leave the country. The second bulletin, asking visitors to Chester Zoo to come forward, was broadcast on all local and national radio and television stations every hour. Just after nine in the evening, D.I. Jones received a call from a man who had been at the zoo that afternoon.

"This is Chris Graham speaking," said the caller. "I heard your appeal on the radio just now. Well, I was at the zoo this morning and, as I was walking from the main entrance back to my car, I noticed something a bit unusual."

"What was that, Sir?" enquired Jim Jones.

"There were three men and a young girl further along the car park and it just seemed that they did not belong at the zoo."

"What made you notice them particularly?" enquired Jim.

"Well, I noticed them because all the other families coming out of the zoo were talking to each other about the animals they had seen, or whatever, but this girl didn't look very happy at all, none of them were talking and they all seemed in too much of a hurry."

"Can you give me a description of the girl?" interrupted Jim, jotting the facts down on the pad in front of him.

"Well, I guess she was medium height and build – perhaps a little on the thin side. She had dark, shoulder length hair and wore jeans and a longish shirt – I am afraid I can't remember the colour."

"What about the men – can you remember anything about them?" queried Jim.

"Only that they were all pretty tall – I would say round about six feet, and one of them was extremely skinny. They all had jeans and t-shirts on," said Mr. Graham, racking his brains to see if he could remember anything else about them. "Oh yes, one of the men had blondish hair," he added. "I wish I could remember more, but when you've got business matters on your mind, it is difficult to focus on what people are wearing."

"I can understand that, Sir, did you see where they went?"

"Yes, they got into a red Ford Mondeo which was parked not very far from where I had my car."

"Did you get any of the registration plate numbers?" asked Jim Jones, elated that they now had a make and colour of car to follow up on.

"Only the letter for the year at the beginning of the plate. I can remember thinking that the car was much younger than mine. Mine's only an R registration, but theirs was a V registration."

"Then what happened?" Jim continued, handing the details of the car to his constable, so that the search for the owner could start straight away.

"I followed them for a while because I was next to them in the line of cars leaving the zoo. When they got to the traffic lights at the end of the zoo road, they turned left and I was going right towards Chester, so I really didn't give it much more thought," replied Chris Graham.

"Can you tell me approximately what time this occurred?" Jim asked.

"Probably about twenty minutes to one," replied Mr. Graham. "I had an appointment in Chester in the afternoon at one-thirty and I gave myself extra time to get there because of the traffic."

"Is there anything else you can remember?" asked Jim.

"No, I am afraid not," Chris Graham said. "I only wish I could have been of more help to you."

"Well, you've given us plenty of details about the car, which will make it easier to trace, and you have also given us a time to work on. If you think of anything else, please let me know as soon as possible, and thank you very much for calling," Jim finished off.

"Of course, that's not a problem," replied Chris Graham and hung up.

After he had replaced the receiver, Jim went to the Records Office to see how his constable was doing with the search for the car and to remind him to pay particular attention to car rental companies. It was unlikely that men like Fingers and The Cat would actually own a car – particularly a bright red one, which might draw attention to them when they were working. Having made sure his constable was hard at work, Jim was thinking about the rest of the evidence Mr. Graham had given them. The girl Chris Graham described must have been Kate. According to the details given by Mrs. Foster and Amanda in their statements, the girl Mr. Graham had described matched in height, build and hair colour and she had been wearing jeans and a long shirt.

Maybe now they could make some progress, he thought to himself as he picked up his notes and went to see Detective Superintendent Richardson.

— Chapter Seven —
Reinforcements

Amanda did not sleep very well. She was extremely restless and unable to concentrate on anything, least of all sleep. Her closest friend was missing and her mind was going over and over all the things she could or could not have done to prevent the kidnapping. Supposing she had refused to go and look for a Security Officer? At least if she had stayed with Kate it was possible that the men would not have kidnapped them if there had been two girls to consider. She was still angry with the security officer at the zoo. She had taken a precious ten minutes trying to persuade him to come back with her to where Kate had remained and even after they arrived there and found Kate gone, he still refused to believe her story. Had he accepted her story right away and gone with her to where she had left Kate, then Kate may still have been around and none of this would have happened.

Then there was the ostrich. Why did the Duty Manager at the zoo deny the existence of the ostrich? Surely he must have known about the bird. Why had this beautiful golden bird also disappeared? Did he have any link with Kate's disappearance? Amanda had noticed that while they were studying it, the ostrich seemed to be looking in their direction, trying to attract their attention. Of course, she had no way of knowing how close her observation was to what actually happened; that indeed Oscar had been focusing on them. It was just a vague notion she had and it kept nagging at the back of her mind.

Giving up on the sleep problem, Amanda got up and dressed. Dawn was still breaking outside and it was too early for her to do anything, so she went for a walk in the quiet village although some of the local delivery people were already about. Arriving home at seven forty-five and before having breakfast she was on the phone to Kate's house to find out if there had been any news of her friend.

"Nothing, so far," said Kate's brother, James, who answered the phone. "Listen, Amanda, I am so worried, can I come over this morning, I need to talk to you?"

"Course you can," replied Amanda. "To tell you the truth James, I can't even think straight and I would also like to talk to someone."

"O.K., see you after breakfast," said James.

Since learning about Kate's disappearance from his mother early Thursday evening, James had gone straight to his computer to see if he could find anything on the Internet which may help them. The only thing that his Mother had been able to tell him was that Amanda had mentioned the names of Fingers and Freddie. James found that there was not a lot of information about criminals on the Net, since material concerning crimes was considered mostly confidential. However, he did find a website 'most wanted men.com' which listed major criminals still at large in the U.K. Although most of the facts were unrelated to his search because the website was devoted mostly to individual hard core criminals, there were additional related websites linked to that one. Eventually, after exploring some of the links, James came across one that included a brief list of well-known and notorious gangs in the United Kingdom. More out of curiosity than anything else, James discovered, when clicking on one of the gang names that a list of individual members of that gang appeared on the screen. He just wondered if the names his mother had given him were related to a gang.

Patiently, James scrolled through the composition of each gang and when he finally came to the Corr Gang, there was the name of 'Fingers'! Feeling a surge of adrenalin, James checked on the history of the gang and found that they had been operating for nearly 16 years. The gang leader was Roger Corr, a criminal with a long record. The Gang's specialty was daring cat burglaries, producing rewards of fabulous value. They had never been caught because the raids were extremely well planned and executed. The police, whilst knowing the Corr Gang had been the perpetrators of the crimes could get nothing on them in terms of substantial evidence that would stick.

Further web crawling did not produce any more information on this 'Fingers' or the Corr Gang, so with a sigh of disappointment James switched off the computer and started to think about the discovery he had made. The more he thought about this, the more he was convinced that the 'Fingers' mentioned as a member of the Corr Gang was the same 'Fingers' that Amanda had identified. While wrapped in thought his mind was unexpectedly invaded almost by a sixth sense that was urging him to go and find Kate. James was puzzled and shook his head in disbelief. He must be dreaming! He tried to dismiss this intrusion but it would not go away. The more he tried to get rid of this definite, compelling feeling the more it came back to him and he started an argument within himself. He had to admit that the whole idea of investigating Kate's disappearance was ludicrous. He had nothing to go on. The only concrete facts he had were that Kate and Amanda visited the zoo and even this was related to him secondhand by his

Mother as had the rest of what he had heard of this unbelievable story.

These same thoughts pursued him the following morning. The fact that by one in a million chance he had been able to find a man by the name of Fingers through the Net, and possibly that this man was a member of the infamous Corr Gang gave him some hope, but it was a very weak link at best. James was now trying to justify a search for Kate, other than she was his sister and he loved her dearly, on the basis of concrete facts. Unfortunately, he had nothing, no pointers, no hunches, and no directions. What he really wanted to do was to jump in the car and drive to Chester. Even if he couldn't do anything else, at least he would be at the scene of the crime. It was while he was contemplating this idea, the telephone rang and it was Amanda.

Because of her close-knit relationship with Kate, Amanda knew James pretty well. The three of them had shared many happy hours together. James and Kate had an excellent brother-sister relationship and James was protective towards his sister. As a result, Amanda had always looked on James as the brother she had never had. Now, at just fifteen, she found that her thoughts of James as a brother were changing. James was now 17 and seemed to have acquired an air of dependable maturity as he was reaching the end of his school years and, of course, he was now driving a car. He was becoming to Amanda something slightly more than a brother, and she would have liked his company a little more often when Kate was not around. She could hardly call it a 'romance', but there was something there because he occupied her thoughts more often than not. Sometimes she would go to the bedroom and stage a fashion show of herself to herself in front of a full-length mirror to see how she stacked up. She was, she decided, not bad! Although she was taller with a larger frame than Kate, by no stretch of imagination could she be called fat. Her short, dark auburn curly hair framed a fair complexion with just a hint of rosy cheeks and the odd freckle. Her big, cornflower blue eyes stared out of dark long lashes, catching her reflection in the mirror.

"Maybe if I wore some make-up," sighed Amanda. She tried to imagine her blue eyes surrounded by thick dollops of mascara and caked eye shadow. Immediately she laughed.

"Not for me, thanks," she replied out loud, "I just couldn't be bothered." This remark echoed perfectly what she thought about herself. Although she was not an outgoing and forward individual when it came to mixing with other people, she had no doubts about her physical appearance as she stood in front of the mirror.

"I am what I am," mused Amanda and decided again that the overall effect was, on the whole, good! Someone else looking on may have decided to comment on her attractiveness and developing beauty.

Back to James, oh yes, he was a super guy – maybe sometime they would have the chance of getting closer to one another, but in the meantime Amanda still did not know what she really felt about James except that she was always pleased to see him and today particularly so, because it meant she could share her feelings with someone of her own age, rather than just her parents.

James, now driving himself, had nearly put his foot through the floorboard of his old jalopy in an effort to get to the speed he wanted. He had scrimped and saved during the past year to buy the old car that was now the centre of his life – well almost! He was a good first time driver because he had been driving within the grounds of the estate for the past two or three years. But his anxiety about Kate and his quest to get more information from Amanda was uppermost on his mind and being somewhat pre-occupied, he forgot to pay attention to the speed limit. Fortunately for him he was not on the main road and generally there are few police who patrol the back lanes of the Welsh countryside, so he made good time to Amanda's place. Amanda was waiting to greet him and the two of them decided to sit out in the sun on the wall rather than go indoors. James felt that he did not particularly want Amanda's mother to hear their discussions and this location was well away from the house.

"Oh, James, I am so glad you came over," said Amanda, "I feel so guilty about what has happened. It is terrible just hanging around at home waiting for the telephone to ring. I have been doing a lot of thinking and quite honestly, I am worried sick about Kate. If only I had stayed with her instead of being persuaded to go and find the security guard, who turned out to be hopeless anyway. If I had been there with Kate, the men might have had more difficulty kidnapping both of us and therefore would not have tried. What I really want to do is to go back to the zoo and see if I can pick up any more clues that would give me a hint of what had happened. After all, I was the person she was with and I know what we both heard and saw. Oh, I know that must sound kind of silly, especially now that the police are involved, but anything is better than just sitting at home doing nothing – I do feel so awful," she added.

"You can forget about feeling guilty," said James. "I know Kate and when she decides that she wants someone to do something – there is no stopping her. Besides, I happen to agree with Kate on this occasion – somebody had to do something. It's funny that you should come up with the idea of returning to the zoo, because I was thinking of the same thing myself. This may sound odd to you, Amanda, and I really cannot explain it properly, but something or someone is 'talking' to me, if you like. I don't hear anything and I don't see anything, but strange thoughts seem to be crowding in on my mind about 'being guided' to find Kate. This happened last night when I had pulled off some information from the Internet on a gang in the U.K. called the Corr Gang. I discovered that one of the gang members was a guy called Fingers."

"That's the same name as one of the men at the zoo was called," Amanda announced excitedly. "True," said James, "but unfortunately that is the only link – a name, and we have nothing further except that the Fingers on the Internet is a member of The Corr Gang. It was after I had finished with the computer and started to think about any possible connection that these thoughts about finding Kate seemed to invade my mind. I cannot talk to Mother and Dad about it because they are so upset at the moment and besides they will probably think I am totally out to lunch. Maybe if we follow up your idea of going back to the zoo we might pick up something. Do you think your Mother will let you go?" he asked.

"She might," replied Amanda with a smile, "if I said that I was going for a short drive with you, but if I told her I was going to the zoo she would go ballistic and never let me go."

"In that case," said James, "we will go for a drive over to the shop in the village as I want to see about getting a computer book – how about that?"

"Hang on for a moment, I'll go and see Mum." With that, Amanda slid off the wall and went to find her Mother to tell her that she was going for a drive with James to the village to pick up a book. Surprisingly, her mother did not have too much of a problem with the idea, but she did remind Amanda that she was off to work shortly and that she was not to be too long because the bread man would be coming that afternoon and an order for bread needed to go in for the next week.

It was not long before James and Amanda had picked up the required computer book and were soon winging their way in James's old car to Chester and the zoo, far from confident that they would find anything, but with the existing situation and their own beliefs pushing them to do something.

If it had not been that he was clutching the steering wheel of his car, Roger Corr would be rubbing his hands with glee at the thought of the incompetent Max possibly facing murder charges and his own satisfaction at the idea of intercepting Fingers and The Cat. He would indeed make sure that those two dirty rats that had double-crossed him, would tell him where the jewels were to be found. After that he would dispose of both of them. Max's stupidity he would allow, but people who double-crossed him would pay dearly. He could not possibly let the Mirendah slip through his fingers. It had consumed his life for the past five years ever since he discovered the existence of the Mirendah and that the Ryerdales had the stone.

This discovery of ownership was quite accidental. A friend of Roger's, Bill Martin, was a concierge in a five star hotel in London five years ago. The Marchioness of Ryerdale had been staying in the hotel for a few days with a friend of hers. The friend had approached Bill for some information on theatre tickets and while Bill was making the call the lady was joined by Lady Ryerdale. The ladies started to chat and the conversation turned to clothes and jewellery and what they would be wearing for an up and coming Charity Ball. It was not a loud conversation, but Bill, waiting patiently on the line for information about the tickets, heard enough of the conversation to realize that the Mirendah stone which the Marchioness was talking about was, in fact, the Diamond.

When he had finished on the telephone, Bill gave the ladies the information requested, and watched as they disappeared through the hotel doors. Bill Martin was not an authority on precious gems but he made it his business to know something about those with significant value so that he could use the information for monetary gain. The Mirendah Diamond was one of these. Smiling to himself, he couldn't wait to sell this particular piece of information to the highest bidder that happened to be Roger Corr.

Roger's planning for the actual theft had been a long, detailed and clever operation. He decided that The Mirendah Diamond was going to be his retirement pension, so he just had to retrieve it at all costs from those two crooks, Fingers and The Cat.

Roger was driving to Chester with Fatty, The Snake and Johnny Graize. He wasn't taking any chances. Fingers and The Cat may have been his best Cat Burglars, but they would be no match for the likes of Fatty and The Snake when it came to a showdown. If necessary, Johnny wielded a hefty blow and Roger was not adverse to using a pistol to silence people, particularly in cases such as this. Time was of the essence because he knew that Fingers and The Cat would not mess around with low bids when getting rid of the diamonds and would, in all probability, be leaving the country after they had received payment. Roger's three passengers sat in relative silence, not wishing to disturb the look of concentration on Roger's face. They had all worked with him for a long time, but like Max, they simply did not know how to read him. One thing was for certain, Fingers and The Cat really had it coming to them and the three thugs rather savoured the job ahead of them.

"Well, Freddie, we finally did it. Good work on your part," congratulated The Cat as the three of them drove back from Chester in the car. They had just picked up Freddie from a marathon all night bargaining session in one of the main city hotels while Fingers and The Cat had been testing their luck at one of the local casinos. After the casino closed they bedded down in the house of another friend who was a first class 'con' artist. While they had been enjoying their good luck in gambling, Freddie had managed to get them up to £10,000,000 for The Mirendah Diamond and the rest of the jewels. When he gleefully told Fingers and The Cat about this, they could not believe their good fortune.

"You didn't say anything about the Bonds, did you?" enquired The Cat of Freddie.

"Nope," said Freddie as he swung into the main road out of Chester towards Chilfray and their rented house. "We just talked about the diamonds, and they will pick up everything tomorrow at the airport in exchange for the money. You will meet in the washroom for the disabled where you will exchange the goods without anyone seeing you. After that you will be free to catch your flight out of Manchester and take your Bonds with you."

"Good," said The Cat. He had not wanted to part with the Bonds because even though they were valuable 'as is', his gut instinct was that they would be worth quite a bit more money in the future. Since the Bonds were Payable to the Bearer, there would be no difficulty in cashing them at any time. How he savoured the future. After a life of crime they were finally going to be able to retire in luxury with everything they ever wanted, free from the dictates of Roger Corr. The Bonds, after all, could wait. With just over £8.5 million received for the jewellery, after paying Freddie his percentage, the money would take care of Fingers and himself very nicely for the rest of their lives!

Fingers and Freddie also harboured a satisfied feeling with their successes. Fingers because he was going to share with The Cat all the returns of the heist and live in luxury, and Freddie because not only had he concluded another successful negotiation which netted him a nice fee, but he would have the pleasure of dealing with and disposing of Kate.

As they by-passed Chester, and swung out to the South towards the zoo, Amanda was watching the car that was overtaking them. "James!" she shouted, "follow that car in front of us – I cannot believe it, those men in the car are the same men who were sitting on the seat at the zoo!"

"Oh I don't believe it," countered James, feeling sure that Amanda had mistakenly identified the men in the car. "Come on, Amanda, here are we on a road out of Chester and we suddenly come across the men at the zoo – get real!"

"James, I am getting real," insisted Amanda, immediately fearing that she was going to have the same trouble with James as she had with the security officer at the zoo. "I tell you, those are the same men - just follow the car, please, James."

"O.K., O.K." said James, now realizing that this was for real. Since they had nothing else to go on, they may just as well follow the car. "But I will have to drop back a little bit so that they do not suspect us following them."

James kept a respectable distance from the other car for another 4 – 5 miles, before they came to Chilfray, to the south of Chester, where the car pulled into a quiet cul-de-sac at the end of the village. James had enough foresight to pull up just before the turning into the cul-de-sac, which fortunately gave him an excellent view of the driveway into which the car had been driven.

"James, we must go after them," said Amanda fumbling for the car door handle and not caring about the consequences, seeing this only as a golden opportunity to possibly find her friend.

"Oh Amanda, don't be ridiculous," replied James. "What could we possibly do? There are three of them and they could well have guns, so what chance would we have? Besides, what are you going to do – walk up to the door, ring the bell and ask them if they have seen Kate?"

"I'm sorry," sighed Amanda as she realized that her rash thoughts would get them nowhere and she angrily brushed her hands over her eyes in order to stem the tears that were stinging at the back of them. James felt sorry for her, and cursed himself for shouting at her. After all, she was the one who was actually with Kate when all this happened and she must be really choked up about everything. His hand closed over hers as he gave it a squeeze of comfort.

"Hey look, they appear to be leaving again," said James, as he watched the three men get back into the car after getting their keys out to open the front door of the house and having a brief conversation. They pulled out of the drive way and drove off, passing James' old jalopy at the end of the cul-de-sac without a hint of recognition for its occupants.

"Oh, thank goodness for that," sighed James, anticipating that they may recognize Amanda, even though she had turned her head away. He didn't have time to think about following them, as the whole move was so unexpected.

"Well, it's probably best if we just sit here in the car and see what is going to be their next move. It's my guess that they are going to be back shortly, because they got their keys out ready to go into the house and then remembered something," reasoned James. "We will wait for a little longer and hope that they do come back. If they don't, then we will go to the police with the information about the house. If they do come back again, we will wait and see what happens and play it by ear." James and Amanda settled down to what could be a long wait.

It had been what seemed like a long night at the police station with nothing much of importance coming in to provide a break for Detective Superintendent Richardson and his men. Apart from Chris Graham who phoned early in the evening and told them about seeing Kate and the three men outside the main entrance to the zoo, there had been no further responses to the message broadcast over the radio and television networks to the public. Also, nothing had been reported back to their Incident Room concerning the All Points Bulletin.

After searching for red Ford Mondeo cars, D.I. Jim Jones had found two people (both women) in the Chester area who owned such cars. First thing in the morning, Jim Jones had dispatched two of his Detective Constables to go and make enquiries about the cars through their respective owners. He didn't hold out much hope for turning up anything. Both ladies in question lived in respectable neighbourhoods, were married and were employed. The description, brief as it was, hardly tallied with the type of men they were looking for. However, no stone was to be left unturned.

Detective Superintendent Richardson, also operating with lack of sleep, wished he could move forensics along so that the tiny fragment of skin caught on the rope would yield further information. He was waiting to find out about the fingerprint match and until he got answers to some of these questions, he had nothing he could move on at the moment. It was disheartening, but he was used to this.

The police had been over the safe in Lord Ryerdale's room with great thoroughness and found nothing that was typical of a robbery. The Corr Gang were so efficient and clever in their work, they never left anything for the police to go on which left any law enforcement agency dealing with the theft, utterly frustrated. Detective Superintendent Richardson harboured a grudging admiration for Roger Corr as the mastermind behind all these clueless heists. The fingerprints and the bit of skin assumed to be left by the murderer, were all they had at the moment and they could not even link those to the Corr Gang. The detective superintendent wished fervently that there had been something more.

John Richardson was very concerned about Kate. She had also disappeared 'virtually without a trace'. The only evidence on that front had been a vague description of Kate, the men who accompanied her and the car. There had been no ransom call for money, which had confirmed that Kate was kidnapped solely for what she had heard. True, Kate had been missing for less than 24 hours, but every hour with no news was beginning to count – seriously. It was made considerably worse by the fact that later in the day he would have to report to Kate's parents about his lack of progress.

Detective Superintendent Richardson gathered his papers together and headed for the Incident Room for his daily staff briefing. His current feeling was that the briefing would be another futile exercise of going over the chain of events yet again without turning up any results.

— Chapter Eight —

On a Collision Course

It was still only six thirty in the morning when Kate settled down in the summerhouse. As she sat and watched out of the glassless window, she suddenly began to feel very weary and tired. After the initial excitement of exploring the house with Oscar, the sleepless night she had after escaping from the hut and travelling with Oscar and Isia, began to tell on her. She realized that she had been up for twenty-four hours without any sleep. Slowly her head dropped and leaning against Oscar's soft feathers, she fell asleep.

Kate must have slept for a couple of hours when she was awakened by Oscar who had heard Isia, perched on top of the roof in an invisible state, warning him of two cars coming in their direction. He pecked Kate gently on the arm and after a minute or two of trying to get her bearings and re-orientating herself, Kate was fully awake and she peeped out over the windowsill of the summerhouse. There was a car parked in the driveway and it was empty, although she could hear distant voices.

The cul-de-sac was deserted except for the old battered car parked just before the actual turn-off to the cul-de-sac. Kate could hardly believe what she saw! That was her brother James' car and it was James and Amanda who sat in the front. She was so overwhelmed with joy that she wanted to run to the car and be reunited with James and Amanda but slight pressure from Oscar reminded her about the other car in the drive. She waited and was planning her next move when she suddenly saw Fingers, The Cat and Freddie appear from the front of the house and go back towards the car, unlock the doors, get in and drive off. While watching the car go, common sense had prevailed and she decided that she could not leave the summerhouse. Any minute the three men might return and that would be the end of all her plans if they saw her. Isia! She must get Isia off the roof and over to the summerhouse.

"Oscar, I need Isia. My brother James and friend Amanda are in that car parked just before the Cul-de-sac, and I must somehow get them to the summerhouse. I have a change purse here in the pocket of my jeans," she added, digging into her pocket to produce the small purse. "Isia could take it to them." As she spoke, she indicated with her hand, pointing first to the roof and then the car and then to herself, hoping that if he could not follow the words, Oscar would understand her arm movements. As it happened, Oscar knew exactly what Kate wanted even without the gestures and he summoned Isia who arrived with a thud on the floor in front of them and then materialized. Kate had to smile when she heard the thud although she saw nothing and then abruptly this wonderful bird appeared before her. It was all so unreal and she began to wonder if she would ever get used to the vanishing and re-appearing acts that went on with Isia and Oscar.

She offered the purse to Isia as she told him what he should do. Isia, of course, already knew this as Oscar had told him. He took the purse gently in his beak and disappeared from the gazebo, only to reappear again on the front of the parked car, frightening James and Amanda out of their skins as he materialized in front of them and folded his great wings neatly down beside his body. They had no idea what this strange, fearsome bird was or where he had come from. James and

Amanda huddled together in the car, not sure what to make of what they saw. Isia waited. He knew what a shock he had caused and was therefore patient, hoping that nobody would come along in the meantime and start staring at him as the Press had done when they first saw him. As he remained motionless, James and Amanda started to relax and James noted the small change purse that Isia held in his awesome beak.

"Amanda, that's Kate's purse he is holding," gasped James, trying to take in everything. "How did this bird get hold of it?" Isia continued to wait because he knew the first step must come from them.

"I don't know," Amanda slowly intoned, "but I think he is friendly or why else would he appear with Kate's purse?" They waited and Isia waited. James was just not sure about the bird. It looked so fierce, but why would it have Kate's purse?

Finally, James slowly got out of the car. As he did, he noted that the bird didn't move. He tentatively offered the flat palm of his hand towards Isia and Isia dropped the purse into James' hand. When Amanda saw this she got out of the car and joined James. The two of them examined the purse.

"It is Kate's purse alright," confirmed James and Amanda nodded in agreement.

Knowing that his presence was now accepted, Isia fluttered down onto the pavement and then started to fly slowly in the direction of the house. He then returned back onto the front of the car and this performance was repeated three times, to the astonishment of James and Amanda.

"James, I am sure he wants us to follow him," said Amanda excitedly, "come on!"

Before James could reply, Amanda was looking at Isia and asking him what they should do now as if she half expected the bird to give her an answer! Isia started to fly slowly towards number 14 and Amanda was following as quickly as she could. James, who did not share Amanda's confidence that this large bird was all that friendly, was not going to let Amanda out of his sight, so he had no choice but to follow her. Isia sailed down the driveway of number 14, down the garden and on to the summerhouse roof. Amanda and James followed. When they arrived at the summerhouse, to their amazement, Kate appeared in the doorway. She threw her arms about her friend and brother and promptly burst into tears of happiness as an astonished but delighted James and Amanda returned her hugs. "Where have you been and what happened?" cried a relieved James, not quite believing that he was talking to his sister.

By this time Isia had returned to his perch on top of the roof of the house, and Oscar had vanished out of sight into his favourite resting place, Kate's pocket. He didn't want to disappear altogether because he wanted to find out why James and Amanda happened to be in Chilfray and what the three of them proposed to do next. He, as usual, had a general idea of what was going to happen, but he didn't have all the details.

"Oh, it is wonderful to see you both again," said Kate. "I must tell you everything but first of all you have to sit on the floor so we won't be seen."

"Did you see the three men drive away?" Kate asked. James nodded as a reply.

"Well, their names are Fingers, Freddie and The Cat," said Kate. "They are the three men who kidnapped me and if they come back to the house and see us, that will be disastrous, so we must keep out of sight."

"I got some information on Fingers from The Net," interrupted James. "Do you know that he is a member of the Corr Gang?"

"Never heard of them," replied Kate. "Tell me more about them."

"They have apparently been around for a long time," explained James, "and they have always specialized in cat burglaries and robberies."

"That makes sense," agreed Kate, "because I am sure they have robbed someone of something. What's more, they are beastly and I think the one called Freddie has a nasty and dangerous temper."

"All the more reason why we don't want to cross them," said James. "Anyway, tell us more about your adventures."

The three of them made themselves as comfortable as possible on the floor of the gazebo and Kate told them what had happened to her. She explained how she had become completely mesmerized by Oscar at the zoo just after Amanda had left to go and find the security guard.

"It was something special," she said, "as if Oscar and I were destined to meet. I really couldn't take my eyes off him, even if I had wanted to. Looking back, I think it was this bond between us that was the signal for Oscar to get out of the zoo."

"What do you mean, 'a signal for Oscar to get out of the zoo'?" questioned James.

"Well, deep down, I have this feeling now that he was actually waiting for me to appear at the zoo, and when I did turn up, he was therefore free to go with me, but for some reason he had to convince me first," Kate continued. "Oh, I know it all sounds wacky, but that is what I really think."

"It sounds pretty crazy to me," sighed James.

Kate went on to explain how Oscar had simply disappeared from his enclosure at the zoo and she had found him nestled in her shirt pocket, just before Fingers, The Cat and Freddie arrived at where she was sitting.

"So really," continued Kate, "Oscar arrived just in the nick of time."

She was very near tears as she told them how Fingers, The Cat and Freddie had forced her to walk with them out of the zoo with a gun held to her back; the awful drive to Chilfray and being tied up in the house. Her sadness turned to anger as she went on to tell them how Freddie had slapped her about the face while trying to get her to tell them what she had overheard outside the ostrich compound.

After her ordeal in the house, there was what seemed like a never-ending drive to Pemberton Forest, her imprisonment and the desperation to get out of there before Freddie returned. She was greatly afraid of Freddie because of his volatile nature. As she related how Oscar had comforted her and helped her, her hands curled over the ball of feathers in her pocket.

"I cannot tell you how I felt to be out of that hut," said Kate, "and I had no idea what we were going to do next or how we were going to get out of the forest. Then Isia landed in front of us and at first it was difficult for me to believe what I was seeing." She went on to relate how she had recognized the friendship between the two birds and how Isia had guided them back to this house because somehow he knew the way. When she explained about her night ride on Oscar's back, Amanda interrupted.

"Kate, how on earth did you stay on Oscar's back?" she asked.

"I found a comfortable place at the base of his neck where I could reach to put my arms around his neck. Oscar was very fast and to get this speed he used long strides, so it was a smooth ride with very little jogging about."

Kate continued telling them about her arrival at the house, how she and Oscar had entered the house and their subsequent search for any evidence to substantiate the theft and discovery of the body. James and Amanda were absolutely astounded that she had managed to survive.

"But why did you come back here?" asked Amanda, "I'm sure that they are going to kill you when they see you."

"The Cat was quite nice to me, but I don't know what will happen when Freddie finds me," replied Kate, dubiously. "I had to come back because I had to try and find out about the body and the jewels. As I mentioned, I think I have discovered something about the jewels, but I still don't know anything about the body."

"Well, in my opinion, it is a good thing that you don't," said James. "Honestly Kate, you are nearly fifteen and you are in a whole heap of trouble as it is, without looking for bodies." James was getting very irritated with his sister because he felt that she should have gone straight to the police instead of riding on the back of an ostrich! "Incidentally, we've seen Isia," said James and we have heard all about Oscar but we haven't yet seen this marvellous bird," added James, with a touch of sarcasm.

"And you won't see Oscar for a little while", retorted Kate, "because he is far too big to fit in here with the three of us, and we must be so careful we are not seen. Besides, James, if you are so miffed with the situation, why do you want to meet Oscar?"

"Quite frankly Kate, I'm having a hard time taking all of this in," said James, starting to lose his patience. "The only fact that keeps me from dismissing this whole wacky story is that I too, had an unexplainable urge to come and find you, so much so that I had to go and see Amanda and try to get some more information from her. Amanda also felt that she needed to return to the zoo to see if she could pick up anything in the way of some small crumb of evidence about your disappearance. While driving to the zoo, we saw this car with three guys in it who Amanda recognized as Fingers, The Cat and Freddie who you overheard at the zoo, so we followed them here."

"So that was when they came back to this house, a short while ago," said Kate, beginning to feel a little ashamed of the way she had spoken to her brother after hearing how concerned he and Amanda had been about her.

"Yes," continued James, "they drove into the driveway and we felt it best not to even turn into the cul-de-sac, so we parked ourselves where you now see the car. As you know, we watched as the men got out of the car, produced some keys and, after a short conversation, they got into the car and drove off again."

"Yes, I saw that, so they really could be back at any minute," said Kate. "We will just have to stay hidden here in the summerhouse for the time being."

"But what are we going to do?" asked Amanda. "We cannot possibly take on those three men – I am sure they would make mincemeat of the three of us."

"Listen," said Kate, "as I mentioned, Oscar and I had a look around the house earlier. What I didn't finish telling you was that in the oven in the kitchen, we found a briefcase which looks and feels as though it could contain a bundle of paper – I guess it could be the Bearer Bonds."

"What?" cried Amanda, "that just makes matters worse – what do you think we will be able to do about these men with some of their loot in the house?"

"Well, I think we can," replied Kate stubbornly. "I hate these men for what they have done to me and for robbing someone else and possibly being involved in a murder. You have yet to see Oscar in action, believe me when I tell you that he is awesome, and I suspect that Isia can be quite a menace with his fierce looks and wicked beak. Between Oscar and Isia these men won't stand a chance. Oscar, I am sure, is my guardian angel and I don't think he will let me get into any serious trouble. When we got out of the hut in the forest, Isia appeared from nowhere and he took a little getting used to, but he seems to know telepathically what Oscar wants him to do. It was Isia who warned us when your car drove up and parked.

I was able to see it from the summerhouse and when I realized it was the two of you, I wanted to rush out and meet you, but I had to remain hidden and it was then I realized that Isia was the one who had to persuade you to come here," Kate finished up with a laugh.

"But Kate, you are crazy," said James. "Why do you want to catch these men personally? You're in terrible danger already and I think it would be far better for us to drive to the nearest police station and hand the operation over to them."

"No," replied Kate, wilfully. "Oscar and Isia will look after me and I just want to see their faces, especially Freddie's, when I confront them myself because they've been so miserable to me. Besides, they said in their conversation that a body had been found and a theft had taken place. If we are able to question them, maybe they will tell us things that will help the police."

"Well," said Amanda, "you will have to have us for company because we are not going to leave you alone again, even if you think Oscar and Isia can help."

"O.K.," sighed Kate, but secretly glad that her friend and brother were going to stay around. "We will all have to just wait here until they come back and I do hope that it will not be too long."

James settled down with the two girls, but he was worried. He thought to himself that these men may be armed and what use would anyone be, including the birds, if guns were produced. He looked again at his sister and Amanda whispering away together and he knew that it was going to be difficult to stop them from confronting the hoods. Thinking about it further, he had an idea – what if he was to go and get the police for backup purposes? After all, if there was a confrontation and if James, Kate and Amanda could overcome these three men with the help of Oscar and Isia, (something James had grave doubts about), the police would be called in anyway. Just as he was about to suggest this tactic, he heard a high-pitched whistle coming from the roof of the house.

"Sh!" said Kate, putting her finger up to her lips, "that's Isia's warning that someone is coming." As she finished her sentence they heard a car pulling up into the driveway. The three of them watched just above the sill as the car door opened and Fingers, Freddie and The Cat got out and headed in the direction of the front door.

"Well!" exclaimed Fingers, as he clutched the local daily newspaper, one of many they had just bought from the local news agent, "we really made a splash with our bit of work up at The Hall."

"It looks as though we made the national headlines too," agreed The Cat as he looked at the front page of one of the national tabloids while negotiating his way through the front door and nearly tripping over the step.

"The mystery remains," said Freddie as he closed the front door behind the three of them, "if you two didn't do it, who the heck did and why did it happen on the same night that you were after the sparklers? Are you absolutely sure that there is no connection?"

"Oh, come off it Fred, we visited this situation in the car – how could there possibly be any connection? The only person we saw all the time we were there was the body."

"Hmm," countered Freddie as he led the way into the lounge. "It all seems very strange and much more than co-incidental – and these headlines don't help us at all!"

"Oh, for goodness sake Freddie, we've got the sparklers and, thanks to you, we've got an excellent price for them. Tomorrow we will be gone and nobody will be any the wiser," concluded The Cat as he separated the pages and gave the front page of the Chilfray Star to Freddie in an attempt to shut him up.

There didn't seem any point in discussing the issue further; Fingers didn't want to get involved in the situation except to savour the journalist's words like 'clever', 'cunning' and 'another clueless heist' which made Fingers feel very good as he interpreted this as a compliment to him. It looked as though The Cat had finally convinced Freddie that they had nothing to do with the murder, so the three of them settled down to read all the newspaper reports.

Listening for the movements of the three men as they got out of the car and went into the house, Kate, James and Amanda heard the faint closing of a door.

"We'll wait for five or six minutes," said Kate, now taking command, "and then we will take them by surprise."

"Don't you think it might be a better idea if we went through the back door? If we go in at the front, we have to pass one of the windows and that just might be our undoing," said James. "Incidentally, where are Oscar and Isia, because we surely cannot go in there without them?"

"Oscar is in my pocket," said Kate, "and Isia will be following our movements from the top of the house. They are past masters at disappearing and re-appearing and when we are in the house, they will appear – that will be the element of surprise and I don't think our three friends in the house will know what to do with themselves. And yes, James, that is a great idea of yours that we go in through the back door because we have cover from the hedge nearly all the way up to the house."

Amanda had to suppress a small giggle as she thought of the ostrich and eagle rounding up the three men. "Serves them right," she thought to herself. Like Kate, she had not really thought everything through, especially what was going to happen if they managed to capture Freddie and his two friends. She knew that ultimately the police would have to come onto the scene. Then she wondered if there was a telephone in the house because James had left his cell phone in the car.

Furtively, the three of them crept out of the summerhouse, flattening themselves against the hedge to avoid being seen as they inched their way up the garden to the house.

James led the way as they crossed over to the back door. He tried the door handle, hardly making a sound as he turned the knob to its full extent. Gently he pushed on the door and thank goodness it opened. Taking one step over the threshold, he paused and listened. He heard voices coming softly from beyond the kitchen and felt quite safe in letting the two girls in. They all stood as a group in the kitchen, straining their ears, hoping to catch what was being said, but it was impossible. Peering into the hall, they noticed that the dining room was next to the kitchen and the room the men were in was beyond that in the front of the house where Kate had been held prisoner. James gently closed the kitchen door to so that they could have a quick planning session and discuss what was the best method of attack.

While all this was going on, Oscar was nestling in Kate's pocket becoming more and more concerned at the attempt of these three teenagers to take on Freddie, Fingers and The Cat. He quickly sent a message to Jenza asking him to come immediately and to station himself invisibly in the garden by the back door. He further explained that it would be better for all concerned if he, Jenza was present. Oscar requested that Jenza go into the kitchen after Kate, James and Amanda had left to confront the men.

Having successfully completed his quest in the desert, Jenza was now back in South Eastern Russia, still very much expecting Oscar to be in touch with him and he was always on the alert. Finally, the message arrived and Jenza needed no second bidding. Oscar had given him the map co-ordinates of the house and Jenza whisked himself from his native land through Russia and Europe to the U.K. It did not take him long to pinpoint the house and he landed safely, unseen, in the garden. Not wishing to arouse any suspicion, he gave a very small cat's mew to let Isia, up on the roof, know that he had arrived. Of course, Isia would have liked nothing more than to fly down to the garden and greet his friend, but he was bound to remain on the roof on guard. He gave one of his soft squeaks acknowledging Jenza and left it at that.

Inside the house, Oscar had transformed himself into his normal size, dwarfing James, Kate and Amanda. Amanda was so pleased and relieved to see him that she tried to give him a hug although not very successfully, as her arms only reached up to the lower half of Oscar's body. However, Oscar knew what she wanted to do and put his neck down so Amanda could rub the top of his head.

James was non-plussed. He had only come across ostriches in pictures and images and in those pictures he recalled, the birds were black and white. He certainly was not prepared for the golden and silver/white-feathered ostrich, which now towered before him, and James himself was 6 feet 1 inch tall. He was speechless but felt the need to put a hand out to touch Oscar in gratitude for the way in which he had watched over and rescued his sister. Oscar in turn, just dipped his head towards James.

"Will we need Isia?" asked Amanda as they prepared for their attack. She still did not understand how the bird was going to get inside the house and just accepted that he would arrive.

"Probably," replied Kate. "But Oscar will send for him when he is needed."

With that, she nodded to James who opened the kitchen door and they crept towards the closed door of the living room, Oscar bringing up the rear.

The homicide team was assembled in the Incident Room to report on their activities. John Richardson walked in promptly at 9:00 a.m. as he always did and the meeting got underway.

Mainly the reports were of evidence that had been sent to various diagnostic services and everyone was waiting for a reply.

Jim Jones explained that two of his men went off this morning to interview the owners of the two red Ford Mondeos, but he didn't hold out much hope for positive results. Just as he was finishing his report, Detective Inspector Barry Bradford burst in through the door, waving a piece of paper. He apologized for being late, but he had been waiting for the information to come through from the Criminal Records Office at the Met.

"I've just heard," he said "we have a positive ID on the finger prints from the doors in the Long Gallery – they belong to Max Melton, one of Roger Corr's henchmen."

"I knew it!" said Detective Superintendent Richardson with a smile. At last, he thought, something on the Corr Gang. "However, let's not get carried away with this. It is conceivable that Max may have committed the murder, but he certainly was not responsible for the heist for he is no cat burglar."

"Since the Corr Gang is involved, I would put all my money on Fingers and The Cat nabbing those jewels and The Mirendah Diamond, so all efforts have to be concentrated on finding those two and they are the ones who have Kate."

Turning towards Jim Jones, Detective Superintendent Richardson requested that Jim round up Max Melton and any other member of the Corr Gang in Manchester, and bring them in for questioning.

"And," he continued, "while we are waiting for the rest of the results, I think we should go and have another look at Ryerdale Hall – see if we can dig up anything else. Barry, can you look after that for me?"

Before concluding, Detective Superintendent Richardson reported to the team that their Assistant Chief Constable had made this case a 'Priority One' and he was prepared to back the team with additional men and whatever equipment was needed.

The meeting came to an end and everyone rose with much lighter hearts than when they had come into the room. Finally, they had a break.

— The Diamond Talisman —

— Chapter Nine —

A Meeting of Great Minds

It was the Friday morning of a long weekend and unfortunately for Roger Corr, The Snake, Fatty and Johnny Graize, they found themselves travelling in the same direction as people who were going for a long weekend to North Wales. For this reason, Roger had expected that the roads would be busy in the afternoon. He had not counted on the number of city people who decided to leave work at eleven o'clock in the morning and turn a three day long weekend into a four day break instead. The Motorway, with three lanes of traffic each way, was the main artery for North Wales and as a consequence of the holiday break, traffic was reduced to a speed of 10 miles per hour in places! Roger was fit to be tied as they crawled along at a snail's pace behind queues of traffic in front of them as well as to the right and left of them. Although the majority of cars belonged to holidaymakers, there were also many semi-trailer drivers anxious to get back to home base before the holiday started.

There was nothing Roger or anyone else could do that would improve matters. Prudently, the three other men sat silently while Roger ranted and raved at the steering wheel.

"Johnny, have a look at the map," barked Roger. "Somewhere up here there is an exit which will take us across country to Chilfray – see if you can find it. Bit longer than the motorway, but if we are going to have traffic like this it will, in the end, be much quicker."

"O.K." replied Johnny as he studied the map, "Yes, here it is, about 2 miles further on, Rog."

"At the rate we're going it is going to take 2 hours just to get 2 miles," growled Roger. It did take a while but they finally got off the Motorway and started out on the narrow twisted lanes of the English countryside, which automatically prohibited any great speed. To try anything more than approximately 30 to 40 miles per hour would mean possibly a head- on smash with something coming the other way, or an overturned car. Occasionally they would get onto a wider, straighter road which would allow an increase in speed, but that was not often enough for Roger who fumed and swore as he drove. His three passengers just sat tight-lipped and white knuckled, hoping they would get to the village in one piece.

Eventually they arrived at Chilfray and it didn't take them too long to find the house, noting the car parked in the driveway.

"Well," said Snake, "it looks as though we are just in time to have ourselves a party!"

"Yes, indeed it does," replied Roger bringing the car to a stop just behind an old jalopy parked by the turning into the cul-de-sac.

"The problem is," went on Snake, "are we going to get in without being seen? If we park the car and walk they will see us approaching the house and if we drive up they will definitely see us – what do you think, Boss?"

"I think we shall go and see if we can find a back lane which runs past the bottom of the house, then we can park the car and go in the back way."

Slowly he pulled out from behind the parked car, past the cul-de-sac and proceeded along that road until he came to the first unmarked left hand turn that was a back entry lane. Turning down this lane it was not long before Roger found the back of the house and a convenient pull-in where he could leave the car.

"Snake, you remain in the car and on the alert – we may need you sooner rather than later for a quick getaway," ordered Roger.

"O.K. Boss," agreed Snake, who was quite content not to get mixed up in the fracas which he knew would result in the house. He hated mayhem and guns and he suspected that Roger would have no hesitation in using his gun if necessary.

What the Gang did not realize was that they were being watched from a position on high at the top of the house. Isia was following every move. He had seen the car arrive and pull up just short of the cul-de-sac and watched the four men talking in the car. As the car started up again, his eyes followed it down the road and into the back lane and ultimately the parking space at the bottom of the garden. He already knew what the situation was in the house, and to his mind these men in the car did not look too friendly and he knew that they would not be welcome in the house. He was just happy to know that Jenza was by the back door and he gave a soft whistle to let Jenza know that they were about to have company.

Jenza, in the meantime, still invisible, had seen the approaching car and removed himself to the side of the garden out of the way of the three men now making for the back door. His instinct, as with that of Isia's, was to stop the men before they got any further, but they both knew that this could cause problems so they would wait patiently until they received word from Oscar.

About two feet away from the back door and three feet from the invisible Jenza, Roger Corr stopped, momentarily.

"You know, Fatty, I could swear something is in this garden other than us."

"Well, I don't see anything," said Fatty, looking around, although he too felt slightly uncomfortable.

"There is a bit of a funny smell, but there is definitely no one around," added Johnny as he eyes swept over the back garden.

"Never mind, it must have been my imagination", concluded Roger as he made for the back door.

As the lounge door opened, Freddie, Fingers and The Cat got to their feet, fully expecting a ghost to appear. To their knowledge there was no one else in the house so who could be coming in through the door? They were even more shocked when Kate walked in, followed by Amanda who they vaguely remembered as the girl who was with Kate, and a tall youth bearing a striking resemblance to Kate.

"What the hell are you doing here?" demanded Freddie, as shock turned to acceptance that it was indeed Kate, and then to complete bewildered rage. He could not figure out how Kate had escaped from the hut in Pemberton Forest, or how she had travelled all those miles to get back to Chilfray. He was beside himself and ready to strangle her and took a step forward. Fortunately, The Cat sensed his mood and put a restraining hand with a vice-like grip on his arm.

"O.K. kid, how did you do it?" asked The Cat, needing to get some explanation from Kate before Freddie exploded.

"Oh, that was easy," shot back Kate cheekily, now brimming with confidence as she stood between James and Amanda knowing that Oscar and Isia were not very far away. "I had help, lots of it," she continued as she turned around and further opened the door for the ostrich. "I would like you to meet my friend, Oscar." Right on cue, Oscar walked into the room and appeared to take up the space of half the room.

The three men sat down again in a complete state of fright and disbelief.

"Wha...at is that thi...ng?" stuttered Fingers, who never, in his small and protected life, had ever seen an ostrich, not even a picture of one. Even when he was at the zoo yesterday, just outside the ostrich compound, he didn't even notice them because he was busy listening to Freddie and how much money he was going to get for the spoils.

"It's only an overgrown bird," retorted The Cat with a degree of fear in his voice, which he could not hide. He was not, at that moment, about to take on Oscar, as he did not like the way the bird was looking at him. Not at all.

Freddie, having recovered from his initial shock harboured no such doubts. The sooner he could get his hands around this ridiculous bird's neck, the sooner they would be free of him. He made a lunge at Oscar. Oscar, of course, had seen the attack coming and without moving, in the matter of a split second, he had reached out with his foot with the wicked claw-like talon on the end of the large toe, had raked it down Freddie's left leg, producing tattered jeans and a large open wound on the leg. Freddie retreated with howls of pain and unmentionable expletives, nursing his injured leg while hopping about on the good leg. James, watching this performance, realized that Oscar could, in fact, do significant damage.

"Now, before I give any more instructions to my friend, Oscar," said Kate, "we would all like to know more about 'the horribly twisted body', 'the sparklers' and 'Miranda'."

"I'm sure you would," said a smooth voice behind her, "I too would like to know particularly about the sparklers and the Mirendah. It is not Miranda, my dear. You thought it was the name of a person. Oh no, this is the fabulous diamond in the rough. I myself organized the, shall we say, expropriation of this gem, together with other diamond, emerald and ruby jewellery, but these gentlemen here," he said, pointing at Fingers and The Cat, "decided to double cross me. Nobody double crosses Roger Corr."   By this time all the colour had drained out of the faces of Fingers, Freddie and The Cat and they sat, motionless like marble statues as they gaped at Roger.

James, Kate and Amanda were surprised by this interruption because they certainly didn't hear Roger, Fatty and Johnny enter the house. Not knowing who the newcomers were, but sensing a fraught and tense situation developing between the three men sitting down and those standing up, Kate introduced herself, Amanda and James, while Oscar kept a wary eye on all the men.

"And I am Roger Corr, my dear, and these are my friends Johnny and Fatty."

"The Corr Gang," gasped James, quite involuntarily.

— A Meeting of Great Minds —

"Yes, that's right," smirked Roger, "the one and only Corr Gang!"

James was now really alarmed. He knew all about the Corr Gang from the Internet and he was fully aware of their capabilities. He knew that they would stop at nothing to get what they wanted. Here he was with the two girls in a confined space with these notorious gang members and there was no way of making a run for it, or, as far as he could see, getting out of the situation. He doubted that Oscar and Isia would be effective now, especially as Roger Corr had a gun protruding from his pocket. "Where the heck is Isia, anyway?" he thought to himself, "Was he in the room invisibly or was he still up on the roof?"

Oscar, in the meantime, was remaining quite still appraising the situation. He knew that the new arrivals were going to present problems and he was far more suspicious of them than he was of the three men sitting down, staring open mouthed at Roger Corr.

"And what do we have here?" said Roger, walking over to Oscar and not quite believing what he was seeing. "I do believe it is an ostrich – yes?" he questioned, turning to Amanda. "What is it doing here?"

"He is my friend," interrupted Kate, "and if I were you, I would watch what you say. If you don't believe what he can do, take a look at Freddie's leg." After inspecting the gaping wound on Freddie's leg," Roger chose wisely to ignore both Kate and Oscar as he walked over to where The Cat was seated. "O.K., Cat. I don't like people who double cross me, especially two people who have been part of my Gang for years and

141

even more especially when it is the most important and valuable operation in our career. Do tell me how you thought you were going to get away with it?"

"Well, you see, Rog..." started The Cat, but he did not get any further because Roger slowly produced the gun protruding from his pocket and Johnny moved across the floor to join him, looking quite menacing. To the left of the door guarding everybody was Fatty with a gleaming revolver in his hand. The atmosphere was murderous and Oscar, without hesitation, summoned Isia and Jenza who appeared instantaneously and pandemonium broke out.

Because of his huge wingspan – nearly eight feet, Isia couldn't really fly in this confined room, so he was reduced to half-flying, half-hopping as he launched himself in Roger Corr's direction and with great ferocity sank his beak into Roger's hand, the hand that held the pistol. Accompanied by a loud wail of pain, the gun thudded to the floor and was retrieved by James who seized the moment while Isia was dodging a blow aimed at him by Roger's uninjured hand. This action galvanized Fingers, The Cat and Freddie who fell onto Roger Corr and Johnny. In a split second Fatty had raised his revolver and was about to fire, but was attacked by Oscar who knocked the gun out of Fatty's hand and then placed his strong two-toed foot over Fatty's feet so that he was not able to move. Fatty's feet hurt like mad and he shrieked in pain. James retrieved the revolver and then gave both pistols to Amanda. He and Kate tried to get hold of Fatty, but it was difficult for them because Fatty was a hefty individual, lashing out at Kate and James even without being able to get away from Oscar. Every time Fatty lashed out, Isia would fly down and sink his beak into Fatty's arm as a reward! Some reward!

Amanda was nervously pointing the two pistols in the direction of the brawl which had developed between Roger, Johnny, Fingers, The Cat and Freddie. She closed her eyes tightly and willed herself to stop shaking. She knew that she would never be able to fire the guns, but she must look as though she could.

Otherwise preoccupied, nobody noticed Jenza standing in the doorway until he emitted the most deafening and ferocious roar. All people in the room became silent as everyone fell away from everyone else. Jenza was in the doorway, Oscar had removed himself from Fatty and stood guarding the window and Isia was perched on top of the sofa just waiting for someone to make the wrong movement. Nobody, however, even thought about this as all eyes were on Jenza as he padded slowly into the room. They gaped at this enormous tiger, lashing his tail and with fire in his eyes. The room now seemed incredibly small. If ostriches were able to register facial expressions, then Oscar's face would have been one of extreme satisfaction and glee at the fear and terror that Jenza was now spreading amongst this group of hoods.

Roger, Johnny, Fingers, The Cat and Freddie, no longer at loggerheads but fearing only for their lives, retreated to the corner of the room in a huddle, knocking over the television set as they pressed into the corner walls hoping, and no doubt praying, that the wall would 'open sesame'. Roger, being the smallest of the five men, was trying to squirm his way beneath the others, but with little success.

This left Fatty, bleeding profusely from his arms where Isia had attacked him, flanked by Kate and James and in a position that seemed to be open prey for tigers.

James' free arm was hugging a very frightened Amanda who was doing her best to control her grip on the two guns in her hands.

Having worked everybody up into a frenzy, Jenza then sank to the ground, looking extremely relaxed as he lay on his tummy, but nevertheless very much alert, his eyes darting here and there, waiting for the slightest movement which might spell trouble. For the rest of the people in the room, the situation was horrendous and fraught with danger, so much so that nobody hardly dared to breathe.

Oscar, with a signal to Isia to take his place at the window, walked over to where Jenza lay, put his head down and brushed his beak over Jenza's head in return for a lick on the beak from the magnificent tiger. Everyone else just stared. Following Oscar's example, although hesitatingly, Kate walked slowly over to where the tiger lay and watched by Oscar, tentatively put the back of her hand in front of Jenza's nose as a friendly gesture towards the big cat.

She had not been quite as terrified as everyone else because she had suspected that Jenza was linked to Oscar, just as Isia was. Jenza offered his friendship to her with a lick of her hand. That, of course, was a signal to Roger Corr that the predicament was not quite as bad as he had thought. "Perhaps, after all, it is a tame tiger," he thought as he straightened himself up.

Kate, who was looking at him, shook her head as if to imply that he should have known better because immediately Jenza was on his feet again with a step and a growl aimed at Roger. Roger sank back and Jenza sat down again a little bit nearer to the five men than he was before.

James was finally beginning to appreciate the special relationship that his sister had with Oscar and subsequently Isia and Jenza. He, too, would have liked to approach the tiger, but something held him back. Jenza was an awesome, magnificent creature and James decided that he should wait for just a little while longer.

"O.K. Kate," said James, "we've got to get the police as soon as possible. I saw a telephone in the kitchen so I will go and make the call, but first of all let's get Fatty here over with the rest of them." James pushed Fatty towards the tiger and this caused Fatty to almost dive into the huddle of the remaining five men, daubing them in blood which was freely flowing from his injured arm.

Leaving Jenza and Oscar to guard the prisoners, James, Kate and Amanda retired to the kitchen, followed by a worried Isia. He landed on the floor in front of Kate and started to pull the bottom of her jeans in the direction of the back door.

"What is it, Isia?" asked Kate, now walking voluntarily in that direction. She opened the back door and saw Isia fly past her. She didn't know where he had gone because she couldn't see him. Within a few seconds she saw Isia take shape again, hovering above a car parked behind the fence at the bottom of the garden. Then he abruptly soared into the sky and returned to his perch on the roof of the house.

Kate quietly pushed the door almost shut and signalled for Amanda and James to join her. They peered around the small opening left by the half shut door.

"So," observed James, "they decided to leave someone on guard — we will have to be careful not to arouse his suspicions."

Kate closed the door and James picked up the telephone and dialed '999'. When the emergency services operator answered, James told her he wanted the police and was put through to the station. After explaining the reason for his call, he was then put through to Jim Jones who happened to be on duty. James gave D.I Jones not only the address of the house, but also the information that the suspects were being cornered by a tiger in the living room. He did not forget to mention that there was a getaway car at the bottom of the back garden.

"What did he say when you mentioned the tiger?" giggled Amanda.

"Nothing," replied James, "but I don't think for one minute he believed me."

Kate bent down, opened the oven door and pulled the briefcase from the large meat pan.

"O.K. you two, I am going to get the key for this briefcase and then we can see what's in it."

Before James or Amanda could stop her she had marched back into the lounge and speaking directly to The Cat, she asked for the key to the briefcase.

"What key, what briefcase?" asked The Cat.

"You know the one I mean," said Kate, "and if you don't give it to me, I shall speak to Jenza," she continued as her hand went down to the tiger's neck.

"Don't you dare give it to her," screamed Roger Corr, as he started to go for The Cat. With one hand gently on his neck, Kate urged Jenza forward and Jenza rose and took a step, with an accompanying growl nicely displaying all his magnificent teeth. That was sufficient for Roger to dive for cover again and for The Cat to yank out a key on a piece of cord from his pocket. As he did this, Kate was sharp to notice that he had a soft leather pouch slung around his waist – and quick thinking prompted her to ask for that too. The Cat rebelled yet again, but another growl from Jenza settled the matter. Gingerly, he offered the key to Kate; terrified that Jenza was going to bite off his hand. He then undid the belt that held the pouch, and handed the pouch over to her.

Kate took the key and the pouch and hurriedly returned to the kitchen, quite happy to leave Jenza to his enjoyable task. The key opened the briefcase and after a gentle shake, out tumbled a packet of papers – the Bearer Bonds.

"Whew," James whistled as he leafed through the Bonds, "there is a fortune here." Kate then gently shook the contents of the pouch onto the table. As the jewels tumbled out, the three of them were stunned. The most they had ever seen in the way of diamonds were their mothers' engagement rings. The necklaces, bracelets, broaches and rings danced with light on the kitchen table.

"Oh, they are gorgeous," gasped Amanda, picking up one of the rings and trying it on her finger. Holding it up to admire her hand, the ring dazzled and sparkled.

"Look, what's in this?" said James, reaching for something wrapped up in tissue paper. As he gently undid the paper, the Mirendah was revealed and James sat down in amazement.

"I guess this is the stone Roger Corr called The Mirendah Diamond," said Kate, her eyes fixed on the glistening pure white light which appeared to shine from the parts of the stone which had been polished.

"It's huge," said Amanda. "It must be worth millions of pounds."

The three of them sat transfixed by the huge stone, which actually looked just like a barnacled rock with the exception of the polished parts, which radiated the brilliance only diamonds can produce.

"I think we had better put all these things back ready for the police when they arrive," said James. They packed away the jewels and the Bonds.

Kate locked the case and gave the key to James for safekeeping and the three of them sat down to wait for the arrival of the police.

When Jim Jones received the 999 call from James Foster, he couldn't believe what he was hearing as he scribbled down the particulars. It sounded as though the Corr gang was about to pass into history. What he couldn't quite grasp, of course, was the mention of a tiger! James had reported all of the criminals were being held at bay by a Siberian tiger.

"A tiger!" exclaimed Jim, he just could not believe it.

"Yes, a tiger, Sir," reiterated James, "named Jenza, although he is not interested in anyone except the criminals." To Jim Jones it sounded as though this whole scenario was from another planet. He wanted to question James further about the tiger, but there really was no time. Assuring James that the police would be there as soon as possible, he replaced the phone.

Gathering everything he needed, he left his office to find Detective Superintendent Richardson. While on the way, he barked instructions over his cell phone to Detective Sergeant Green to organize the armed response team to rendezvous with him at Chilfray as soon as possible. When Jim arrived at Detective Superintendent Richardson's office, it mattered not that John Richardson was briefing the Chief Constable on the murder and kidnapping investigation under way. As he swung open the door, Jim excused his interruption and promptly presented his news.

The Chief Constable smiled, "Well, John, it sounds as though you have your work cut out for you and you don't need me around. I will be going and you can give me a call later today."

On the way to the car Jim explained the rest of the news to John Richardson.

"You mean to tell me that there is a tiger in the equation?" he asked, looking astonished. "That's bloody ridiculous – you don't have tigers guarding prisoners! Where did it come from – the zoo?"

"To tell you the truth, Sir," said D.I. Jones, "I don't know and as time was at a premium, I felt that the sooner we got an armed response team together, the better."

"Quite right. Well, if we have to take on a tiger in addition to the rest of the mob, so be it. I trust that you have organized sufficient men, as well as the armed response team?" Detective Superintendent Richardson enquired.

"Oh yes," replied Jim. "They are all on their way to Chilfray. James mentioned that one of the gang was waiting in the back lane ready for a quick getaway, so one of our cars will be going there directly."

"Good work, Jim - except for the tiger," John Richardson added, looking concerned. "All we can hope is that no further trouble has broken out before we get there. Has Barry already gone?"

"Yes, Sir," replied Jim as he held the door open for the Superintendent, got into the car himself and set the siren and blue flashing light going.

The two men lapsed into silence as they drove as fast as they dared along the country lanes to Chilfray. John Richardson was thinking about the Corr Gang – was he going to gain the prize that every police force in the land wanted – the final arrest of the Corr Gang? He dared to hope.

— Chapter Ten —

The Matter is Settled

Within about 20 minutes the police arrived at Chilfray and went straight to the house. As arranged, one police cruiser went on past the cul-de-sac, turned into and blocked the lane leading to the back of the house to scotch any chance of the car and driver making a quick getaway. Waiting for D.I. Jim Jones and Detective Superintendent Richardson on the front driveway was James with Detective Inspector Barry Bradford.

While waiting for the Superintendent to arrive, Barry Bradford had gone with James into the house to assess the situation. He did not want any shots fired just because there was the tiger and his men would naturally be afraid of it. While assessing the situation, which he found quite unbelievable, Barry was able to re-assure himself that guns were unlikely to be used. He explained all this to Detective Superintendent Richardson and James added that there was also an ostrich that was guarding the window and a bald eagle on the rooftop, acting as a lookout. The men glanced up curiously to the roof of the house, having no idea what a bald eagle was supposed to look like, but they could see no sign of anything on top of the roof. At that moment Isia had chosen to remain invisible which infuriated James, seemingly making a liar out of him.

"He's probably in his invisible mode and that is why you cannot see him. All three creatures have a habit of appearing and disappearing," added James in a very matter-of-fact voice as though the practice of invisibility was a regular and known occurrence. He turned to the Detective Superintendent who was obviously looking for some further explanation.

"Sir, neither the birds or the tiger will hurt your men - in fact Jenza, the tiger, will probably bring the prisoners to your cars for you," grinned James. "The prisoners don't stand a chance and they know it," concluded James. D.I. Bradford nodded in agreement and produced the two hand guns that James had taken from Roger and Fatty. He added that he thought that there was probably another gun with the guy waiting in the car at the back of the house.

"A couple of my men have already taken care of him," replied John Richardson, "but I must say, James, that you and your friends seem to have done all our work for us." He grinned at James trying to hide the fact that he was utterly puzzled by everything he had been told and part of him rebelled against believing what James or D.I. Bradford had said. It was just too much. Erring on the side of caution with a tiger to consider, Detective Superintendent Richardson turned to Barry Bradford and suggested that the best policy was to leave most of his men outside surrounding the house while the two of them, would go in and bring everyone out.

By this time, the local people who had heard and seen the police cars arrive, were starting to gather outside the house, anxious and curious to know why not one, but three police cars, plus a police van, were at this particular address. They tried to pump the police officers for more information but were met with stony silence and this left the crowd more curious than ever.

Detective Superintendent Richardson opened the front door and Barry Bradford led the way to the room where everyone was congregated. As they opened the door, what a sight greeted them. Roger Corr, Johnny, Fatty, Fingers, Freddie and The Cat were all huddled together in the corner of the room, held at bay by this massive tiger which was only about two feet from them all. Nothing in John Richardson's training or subsequent career had prepared him for dealing with a roomful of criminals and a Siberian Tiger and he began to feel slightly uncomfortable in spite of James' reassurance that the tiger would not be a problem. Barry Bradford too was feeling anxious now that he was actually standing next to Jenza, and was shifting from one foot to the other in a rare display of nerves, although this would not have been apparent to anyone watching. The two detectives were so focused on Jenza, that they failed to notice Amanda as she went over to Detective Superintendent Richardson and greeted him warmly, most thankful to see him.

"Oh, hello Amanda," said John Richardson as he finally took his eyes off the tiger, looked at Amanda and smiled. "I am glad to see that you are quite safe. This young lady must be Kate – yes?" he enquired, acknowledging her as she stood by Oscar.

"Hi, Superintendent," greeted Kate, and then she continued, "you musn't mind Jenza, he is only concerned with those men in the corner. Oh, and this is Oscar, who has really been looking after all of us."

The two detectives felt that their heads were enveloped in a thick fog as they tried desperately to understand this unbelievable scenario being played out before them, and yet they were forced to recognize that it was actually happening. Detective Superintendent Richardson had, therefore, to accept Kate's assurance that Jenza would not do any harm to them, but that did not bring him much relief.

Signalling to Don Bradford, the two police officers walked over to the huddled bunch of men, giving Jenza a wide berth, pulled Roger Corr upright, pinned his arms behind his back, and slipped handcuffs on him with great satisfaction while cautioning him. Barry Bradford then proceeded, methodically, to arrest each man, handcuff and caution them. Jenza's periodic low growls ruled out any kind of resistance.

"O.K.," said Detective Superintendent Richardson, addressing The Cat – "where are the jewels?" The Cat remained silent, but Kate immediately came to the rescue and volunteered the information.

"I know where they are, Detective Superintendent, I'll go and get them for you." With that Kate ran off into the kitchen, retrieved the briefcase from the oven pan and returned with a triumphant look on her face, presenting the briefcase to John Richardson. "James has the key to the briefcase in his pocket," she added.

This was getting beyond the Detective Superintendent. What should have been an exceedingly difficult arrest was all going so smoothly and everything was being handed to him on a plate, so to speak, by teenagers!

"Well done, Kate," said the Detective Superintendent, "you and your team have certainly done an excellent job."

"Well, m'dear," sneered Roger, a look of pure hatred spreading across his face as he looked at Kate, "I hope you are satisfied with your work today. Before I go, let me tell you that you and your friends will pay dearly for this, believe you me," he said in a menacingly threatening voice, as his look of loathing now included Amanda, James, the birds and Jenza.

"That's quite enough, Corr," said Detective Superintendent Richardson curtly. "Now, get going. Kate, do you think Jenza might accompany these gentlemen to the car?" he added with a grin.

Kate looked at Oscar and then Jenza who knew exactly what he was going to do anyway. The strange procession with Richardson and Bradford leading the way, followed by six handcuffed men, trailed by Jenza and Oscar with Kate and Amanda and other police officers bringing up the rear, walked out of the front door towards the waiting police cars.

As the tiger appeared behind the prisoners, the small crowd that had gathered to find out what was going on did a double take. This was just not possible, was the general terrified thought, but as Jenza continued to herd the prisoners into the van, the small crowd quickly disappeared!

"Oh, good," said Kate to Amanda, "at least we don't have to explain about Jenza."

John Richardson approached James for the key to the briefcase, which James willingly supplied.

"James, I will obviously be needing statements from all of you," he said, "but it can wait until tomorrow morning. We will get this little lot safely into custody first! Have you got transportation home?"

"Oh yes," replied James, "my old banger," he announced with pride, pointing out his car to Detective Superintendent Richardson.

"Good. So will you please come to the police station tomorrow morning at about ten thirty?" queried Detective Superintendent Richardson.

"Yes, that'll be fine," said James.

"Well, I'll leave you in peace with er-hm-your menagerie. I really should take the tiger back with us, as it is illegal to have the beast on the loose. Where did you get him from - Chester Zoo?" He made this statement half seriously and half in jest. He certainly had no idea where the tiger had come from, if not a zoo, and he seriously wondered how the police would be returning it to the zoo or wherever. He was therefore extremely relieved by James' next statement.

"Don't worry about Jenza, Sir," replied James, "he will be leaving with us and my father will be arriving to take charge of him," he lied.

"Oh, very well then," said John Richardson, deeply relieved. "I will get Detective Sergeant Green to keep an eye on things until your father arrives."

"Goodbye, James, bye Kate and Amanda - see you tomorrow," said Detective Superintendent Richardson, as he turned on his heels, thankfully.

"Bye, sir," replied James, followed by a similar remark from the girls. He felt so guilty about lying to Detective Superintendent Richardson, but he could not risk Jenza being taken away by the police. He didn't know where Jenza had come from, but it certainly was not the zoo and he also knew that there was something special about Jenza.

A couple of the police cruisers left with the Core Gang while the police van sped away with Fingers, Freddie and The Cat leaving Detective Sergeant George Green and a few uniformed men to seal off the house ready for forensics to come and gather what evidence they could find which would help to convict the Corr Gang.

Kate glanced furtively around and could see several people peeping through curtained windows of some of the houses on the cul-de-sac, and she promptly went to D.S. Green.

"Detective Sergeant Green," she said, "would you mind very much if I took a few moments with my friends in the house before you finally seal it?"

"Well, now, it is highly irregular, but since these are very special circumstances, O.K., you can have ten minutes," replied George Green. He was actually quite relieved that Jenza would be going into the house and was prepared to make any kind of concession to see that happen. He also hoped fervently, but he thought in vain, that Jenza would not be coming out of the house. Kate turned to James and Amanda.

"I think we had better get inside," suggested Kate, "before Jenza arouses any more curiosity and she led the way into the house. Isia, who had overseen the departure of the police and prisoners from his perch on high, re-appeared with them in the living room.

"Oh, Oscar, Isia and Jenza," said an emotional Amanda, "I don't know whether you can understand this, but you saved our lives and I am pretty sure of that – a big thank you."

"Yes," agreed James. "I don't understand why you are here or where you have come from, but without you we would have been in big trouble."

Kate, too choked to say very much, whispered, "Thank you," as she gave Jenza a gentle hug, patted Oscar and stroked Isia's neck feathers.

James went to the phone in the kitchen to contact their parents and to bring them up to date with the news. He also confirmed that they would be home in about one hour. Returning to the lounge, James asked, "Kate, what will happen to Oscar, Isia and Jenza?"

"I think Jenza and Isia will take care of themselves after we've gone," said Kate, knowingly, "but Oscar will come home with me."

"What do you mean, Oscar will come home with you – don't be silly Kate, you cannot possibly take a fully grown ostrich home in the car, besides, what on earth will Mum and Dad say when you tell them you have acquired a pet ostrich?"

"There will be no problem taking Oscar home in the car," assured Kate, "and I don't think Mum and Dad will mind me keeping him, once they and you know the full story behind all this."

"I must say that will all be very interesting," said James, "when we actually get to hear the whole story," he added, teasing his sister. "But I still don't understand how you are going to transport that bird in the car?"

"You forget James, I told you that he travels in my pocket," said Kate as she rubbed Jenza's back and stroked Isia around the neck. "Thanks again, you two," she said, and was rewarded with an affectionate rub against her leg by Jenza's head and a gentle nibble on her ear from Isia. Knowing that they would shortly disappear, Kate made for the front door, very sad at leaving them. Also acknowledging the tiger with a pat, and a scratch for Isia, Amanda and James followed Kate and Oscar outside and was surprised that once outside, Oscar was nowhere to be seen.

"Where's Oscar gone?" demanded Amanda.

"Back into the pocket of my blouse," replied Kate with a smile.

"Oh," sighed Amanda, who had been rather looking forward to driving through Chilfray and back home along the expressway, with one huge ostrich peering out of the sunroof!

Going to the front room window and looking through, James wanted one more look at the tiger and the eagle before leaving, but the room was empty. Jenza and Isia had gone and somehow he had known that they would be gone. He decided not to say anything as he waved good-bye to D.S. Green, assuring him that the tiger had 'disappeared' and hurried to catch up with the girls.

"Was it all a dream?" he wondered out loud as he walked to the car. Then he realized that no, it was not a dream, because the police had been there and a small team of uniformed men, led by D.S. Green were still sealing off the house. The police had seen the birds and Jenza and they had captured six criminals with thanks mostly due to the tiger – but still James had difficulty. A tiger and a bald eagle do not just appear in the Village of Chilfray nestled on the border between England and Wales. "Were they real? Did it all happen? How could they possibly prove it without Oscar, Isia and Jenza?" Isia and Jenza had gone, and there was no sign of Oscar. As he unlocked the car for the girls and before getting into the back of the car, Kate put her hand into her pocket and pulled out a miniature Oscar.

James looked at Amanda and then Kate and finally his eyes came to rest on the small ball of fluff in Kate's hand that was indeed Oscar.

Slowly nodding his head, "Yes, it did happen."

When they arrived home at The Hawthornes in the late afternoon, they were greeted by two sets of very anxious parents. Marianne and Mark Foster were relieved beyond belief that their daughter had returned to them full of beans and totally unharmed. After hugs of joy all round, Marianne led the way to the lounge where she had tea and crumpets ready for everyone. When she saw the look of disappointment on James' face, which indicated that he had not eaten since breakfast and crumpets were just not enough, she assured him that she was cooking another meal which would be ready in about one and a half hours.

Over tea, Kate repeated her story, which was embellished here and there by James and Amanda. Just as James had done, Marianne, Mark, Brian and Justine had great problems believing that Oscar, Isia and Jenza actually existed. After much persuasion, they accepted it as being true, especially since they recognized that all they had to do was to ring the police for confirmation. However, the general drift of the conversation and the reluctance of her parents to accept the parts the animals played in the drama discouraged Kate from introducing Oscar at that particular time. It would have to wait until later, after Amanda and her parents had left.

— The Matter is Settled —

The excited chatter and explanations died down towards the end of the afternoon and it was time for Mr. and Mrs. Thompson and Amanda to return home. Amanda, of course, was most disappointed that Oscar was not going to appear, but she understood her friend's decision about this. Before leaving, it was agreed that Mark Foster would pick up Amanda the following morning so that they could all go to the police station to make their statements.

Later in the evening, while James and Kate were talking about Oscar and what he had done for all of them, Kate put her hand into her blouse pocket and produced the small ball of feathers.

"Mummy and Daddy," she said as she turned to her parents, "this is Oscar." She opened up her right hand to reveal the bundle of feathers. Oscar perched on her hand, waiting for a signal from Kate that he should revert to his normal size. He recognized the lack of credibility he had with Kate's parents and had already decided he would be guided by Kate in this matter.

James, for a brief moment, smiled and wished that he had a camera to record the stunned look on the faces of his Mother and Father as they peered at Oscar. When Kate suggested that Oscar become his normal size, they were unable to speak but nodded their approval. As they saw Oscar transform himself from the small bundle of feathers in Kate's hand into his regular, large size and stand looking down on them with his enormous eyes and soft halo of white fluff around his head, their parents just sat there and gaped in silence.

It became obvious to James and Kate that although their parents had supposedly eventually accepted the participation of Oscar, Jenza and Isia in their adventures, this was only lip service on their part. Now, as they looked up at Oscar, they had no alternative but to accept that their daughter had a new and very protective companion, Oscar!

He just took their breath away.

Struggling with Oscar's huge presence, Marianne said, "He is quite beautiful," as she looked at his golden colour, shimmering white down on his neck and head and the most extraordinarily beautiful eyes.

"Yes, he is rather a splendid specimen," agreed Mark.

"Well, he is not going back to the zoo," said Kate, "he will remain here with me."

"Now look here, young lady," Mark reprimanded his daughter, annoyed that she had already decided on Oscar's fate without consulting them. "Oscar has a proper home and it is at the Chester Zoo. In fact, when we go to make the statements tomorrow, we will take Oscar with us and return him to the zoo."

"You can't do that," cried Kate. "Listen, Daddy, Oscar is very special and I think he is here because he is my guardian angel."

"That is a little far fetched, dear," argued her mother, "I mean, I think there are guardian angels, but they usually are people, not birds or animals." Then she suddenly remembered the conversation between Amanda and the zoo duty manager about the ostrich. "To tell you the truth Mark, Kate may have a point, because Amanda told the zoo manager that the golden ostrich was missing and he flatly denied that there had ever been such a bird at the zoo. If that is the case, then it would seem that Oscar had the choice and ability of being at the zoo only when it suited him."

"Mummy," said Kate, "I used to sit on that big old stump just off the driveway up to the house. Each time I did, I looked at the sky and ended up with an odd feeling, which was neither good nor bad. It was as if something would happen in the future and I really believe it has – Oscar!"

"Mum and Dad," waded in James, "how about letting Kate keep Oscar for three months?" I have to admit that if Oscar had not been with Kate over the last couple of days, then Kate might not have been with us now. I have seen Oscar in action and he is brilliant!"

This discussion went on for a while with all the pros and cons being put forward concerning Oscar. Finally, Mark agreed that Kate could keep Oscar for two months, but not in the house in his fully-grown state. She was to be solely responsible for him and it was up to her to keep him out of any kind of trouble!

"Since I cannot logically explain why he can transform himself from small to large and vice versa, and some of the other events you have told us about, I think you might be right that there is something special about Oscar, so we shall just have to wait and see. I am not prepared to discuss this matter further, except to say that he is a very handsome bird," conceded Mark. Oscar sealed his approval of this compliment with a bow of his head, causing a hint of a smile to cross Mark's face.

Kate was so happy she gave everyone a big thank-you hug and decided that to celebrate, she and Oscar would go for a walk, with Lulu, of course.

A couple of weeks following the safe return of Kate, James and Amanda, Mark and Marianne Foster with James and Kate (and Oscar in the designated pocket), Brian and Justine Thompson with Amanda, plus Detective Superintendent Richardson and his wife were all guests at a dinner given by Andrew, Marquess of Ryerdale and the Marchioness.

Each of the occupants of the different cars going to the Hall that night felt a tinge of eagerness. They drove up the winding driveway to Ryerdale Hall to discover a magnificent, fairytale castle at the end of their journey and their anticipation grew. The Hall was bathed in floodlights, so there was no problem in finding the main door. Lord Ryerdale was there to greet them at the top of the impressive flight of stone steps and once inside, Elizabeth, Lady Ryerdale, greeted them. Within the forbidding presence of the Hall, the guests almost expected to see Lord and Lady Ryerdale wearing evening dress and jewels, but, in order to make their guests comfortable, they were dressed informally, as was everyone else.

The Marquess felt that he owed a debt of gratitude to Kate, Amanda and James. After they had been stolen, he was convinced that he would never see his precious jewels again, least of all the Mirendah and miraculously, these teenagers had ensured that eventually the Mirendah, the jewels and the Bearer Bonds would be returned to him. He was exceedingly grateful.

To the Marquess the jewellery represented bits and pieces of his family life over the past 400 years. Each piece of jewellery could be traced back to the original owner. There were portraits of all those owners and their wives adorned with the appropriate piece of jewellery, hanging throughout the rooms and corridors of Ryerdale Hall. He also enjoyed seeing his wife wearing the jewels at formal and state functions.

As for the Mirendah – he had mixed emotions about that stone. Some days he felt that he would like to return it to its rightful owner, which would be problematical because there is no longer a Sultan of Mirendah or a traceable family belonging to the Sultan. The best he could consider was returning it to the Government of India.

Lord Ryerdale could now see the folly of his ways, by not insuring the Mirendah and jewellery and not sharing the location of his safe with the police. He could afford but was not prepared to pay the astronomical insurance premiums for The Mirendah, so he had decided to remove it to the bank for ultimate safe keeping when it was returned to him. The remainder of the jewellery he would have insured and the police would be informed of every place of safekeeping in the Hall.

The dinner party had been good and enjoyable with lots of talk, chatter and camaraderie. Detective Superintendent Richardson brought them all up to date with the fate of the Corr Gang who had been arrested in Chilfray with Freddie. They were on remand with no possibility of bail. In all likelihood a trial will be held within the next few months and, hopefully, the members of the Gang in custody will be convicted. John Richardson confirmed that if they are found guilty, which they probably will be, simply based on the evidence to be given by Kate, Amanda and James, they will be sentenced to a long time in jail.

Max Melton had been apprehended in Manchester for the murder of Burt Manley and, if convicted, he could be sentenced to life imprisonment. Unfortunately, two of the gang members, Alan Corr and Joey Lang, are still at large and the police can find nothing. John Richardson admitted that they are not worried about Joey Lang, but Alan Corr is Roger's son and will have to be watched as he can definitely cause trouble in the future.

It had been on Kate's mind to discuss Oscar and the zoo with John Richardson because the story about the zoo manager denying any knowledge of the bird had caught her by surprise. Then, as she thought about it, she had second thoughts. If the zoo says it does not have a golden ostrich, then so be it, thought Kate to herself, and put the idea of the zoo right out of her mind.

After dinner, when they were all having coffee in the drawing room, Kate, James and Amanda asked Lord Ryerdale if he would tell them a little more about the history of the Mirendeh Diamond Talisman.

The Marquess was happy to do this. He got up and went over to a portrait of Cecil, Lord Ryerdale hanging on the wall behind the couch and introduced Cecil to the company present. Andrew Ryerdale then started telling the story of how Cecil acquired the diamond. He got so wrapped up in relating the story that his young and older audiences alike were captivated. Even Lady Ryerdale had not heard the full story before from beginning to end. When he got to the part where the outlaw band was racing towards the train in order to steal the diamond, a strange thing started to happen.

The sun had almost set and its last red rays poured through the window onto Cecil's portrait. But Cecil was no longer there. An affluent looking gentleman with swarthy skin, resplendent in silk clothes, had replaced him. On his head was a silk jewel-encrusted turban secured above his forehead with a plume of enameled gold set with precious gems surrounding a large sapphire. The attire of the man in the picture suggested that he was a Sultan! As the sun's rays finally died, the lights in the drawing room flickered eerily. Then the gentleman in the picture seemed to smile and cast his arm and hand in a giving gesture towards the Marquess.

Just as quickly as all this had started, everything returned to normal. It was Cecil in the picture, looking just as he had looked when they first saw him and the lights no longer flickered. The Marquess cleared his throat and carried on with his story just as if nothing had happened. Although they were all a bit unnerved, the seated company composed itself again and tried to pick up the remaining threads of what the Marquess was saying. When he had finished, everyone remarked on how interesting it had been. Only Kate came right out and asked what had happened in the middle of the story.

"Oh, that," said Andrew Ryerdale, "you should just ignore it. We have odd things like that happening in the Hall from time to time. Now, who would like some more coffee?" Gradually the atmosphere lightened up and the talk went back to Oscar, Isia and Jenza and recent events. When the clock struck ten, Mark Foster suggested it was time they were taking their leave.

"Just before you go," said Lord Ryerdale, "when this whole mess has been sorted out, I would like you, Kate, James and Amanda to be my guests on a trip to my holiday home on Grand Bahama Island, just off the Florida Coast. I might add also that it is very close to Disney World. I cannot repay what you have done for me, so I hope you will accept this holiday as a token of my appreciation."

"Oh, will we ever – that's just brilliant!" chorused the three of them in unison.

As he lay in Kate's pocket, Oscar saw the possible holiday from an entirely different angle. It would certainly be no holiday for him! That is another story.

THE END

Another Exciting Novel

If you enjoyed *The Diamond Talisman*
you won't want to miss
Susan Lancaster's
exciting new novel about Kate's
unexpected and mysterious adventure
in the Bahamas

The Caves and the Skull

When and why did events start to go horribly wrong?   Kate, Amanda and James had been looking forward to a perfect holiday on Grand Bahama Island, but matters soon took a sinister turn when they visited Doge Island and found that it was not all that it appeared to be.   Even the two new friends they made on the Island could not eradicate the peculiar feelings James and the girls harboured about Doge Island. The five youngsters began to encounter bizarre events which made them feel that that they are on the outer ring of a whirlpool, spinning closer and closer to the vortex with no way of stopping themselves.

Ultimately, James and Raoul are captured with no hope of escape and the girls are left to fight off the evil forces that seem to surround the island.   The resources of the ostrich, eagle and tiger are stretched to the limits and without co-operation from the terrified islanders, Oscar, Isia and Jenza must do their best to stabilize an extremely dangerous situation.

There seems no way to prevent the inevitable which will involve everyone in a formidable adventure with masters of the underworld and international syndicate warfare, all playing for the highest of stakes – control and money.

Disaster looms unless the operation uncovered on Doge Island is stopped.

You may order from our website:
www.snosrappublishing.com, or

contact us at: info@snosrappublishing.com

About the Author

After a successful career in business management, cut short by a disabling accident, Susan Lancaster turned to writing full time. Her book *The Frog Snogger's Guide* is a guide to a better and easier life, both at home and at work.

Wanting to distance herself from business and firmly believing there is a child in each one of us, she set out to write stories for young adults that provide a means of entertainment and escape from the realities of this world. Since writing *The Diamond Talisman,* Susan has written *The Caves & The Skull.* She is currently working on another book, *Hell's Gate,* which will be available later this year.

Susan resides on Vancouver Island in Western Canada with her husband, Denis and their dog, Jesse.